MAGNOLIA BLOSSOMS

Book 2

Reggie Chronicles

By
Lynda Rees

Magnolia Blossoms

Reggie Chronicle 3

By

Lynda Rees

Email: lyndareesauthor@gmail.com
Website: http://www.lyndareesauthor.com
Original Edition
Copyright © 2022 by
Publisher: Sweetwater Publishing Company
6612 Ky. Hwy. 17 North, DeMossville, KY 41033
http://www.sweetwaterpublishingcompany.wordpress.com

TABLE OF CONTENTS

Magnolia Blossoms

Magnolia Blossoms

DEDICATION:

*This book is dedicated to dear friend,
Lola Parsley.
Thank you for blessing me
with the gift of you in my life.
Our time together,
whether frequent or less is
not nearly enough.
You are so special to me.
You are family, friend,
and my angel friend.
I appreciate the fun we've shared.*

*Love you, always,
Lynda*

CHAPTER 1

FBI Agent Reggie Montgomery and her best pal, Lemon Sage Gordon stood behind the curtain in a press room of the Sweetwater television station.

"Thanks for coming with me today, Sage. As Department Liaison it's good of you to stand in for the sheriff. We need the parents to remain as calm as possible during the investigation. Having a show of force behind the search will help. They need to understand we're doing everything possible."

Sage shrugged. "Not sure what good I'll do, but I'm happy to be here. Wyatt's been working ten-hour days for three weeks straight. He needed this time off, and he and Shae have had their hunting trip today planned for months. Deer season is extremely short. I didn't want him to skip it."

Reggie laid a hand on Sage's shoulder. "You're a good wife. It takes a special person to live the life of a sheriff's wife."

Sage smiled. "I guess that's something you and Shae don't have to worry about. With you both in law enforcement, you understand stress that comes with the job."

Reggie frowned. "Yes, but still, the hazards of our careers affect our lives. This is anything but a vacation. I was hoping Shea would get some rest while we're here."

"Yeah, I know. You and Shae wanted to spend this week with friends. It's good for Wyatt, though, that your boss asked you to step in and take over the FBI's end of this missing child case."

"Yeah, Benson was called away on another case. Lucky I was in town."

Larry Benson had replaced Reggie on the Sweetwater Human Trafficking Task Force when she and Shea had been reassigned. Now he had been pulled into an undercover case. Reggie had stepped into her previous role—the one she'd give her eye teeth to return to permanently.

"Shae has no lasting effects from his injury. Guess the surgery and therapy helped him fully recover." Sage eyed her curiously.

Mumble of the crowd of reporters on the other side of the curtain grew louder. They were getting antsy. It was nearing time for the press conference.

Reggie glanced at her watch and nodded. Her fingers raked the stone she always wore around her neck. "That and his stubborn will. The man's a fiend when it comes to working out. He's back to his old self, maybe even stronger."

"That's a good thing. A U. S. Marshal needs to be in top shape." Sage slid a hand along her best pal's arm. "So, if you and Shea could, would you move back to Sweetwater?"

Reggie sighed, heavenward. "In a heartbeat. We feel useless in Utah. Utah . . . for God's sake! Nothing important happens in Utah. We'd give our eye teeth to be reassigned to our last post in Sweetwater. We're not being punished, only pushed into the twilight zone until the public forgets our way-too publicized faces."

Sage snickered. "Well, you have to admit. You had the wedding of the century. It's taken years for people to stop talking about you."

"Yeah." Reggie grimaced. "We were supposed to keep a low profile, so we could be effective at our jobs. Shea and I have a passion for that work. We want to get back to it, and we want to live close by our friends. We'd take positions anywhere in the Midwest, within driving distance of Sweetwater, so we could be near you, Wyatt and our friends."

"We miss you and Shea, too." Sage's head turned toward the back hallway. "Here come the parents." She gestured toward the mid-thirties couple entering the back door.

Reggie walked toward the couple and shook the hand the man put forth. "Mr. and Mrs. Moore, how are you holding up?" Sage followed Reggie into the hallway.

Twila Moore winced. "Good as you expect, I guess. Nervous." Her husband, Ryan, slipped an arm around her.

Reggie put a hand to the mother's wrist. "That's to be expected." She gestured toward Sage. "This is my associate from the Sheriff's Department, Sage Gordon."

Sage extended a hand and shook the man's when he offered it. "I'm sorry to meet you under these circumstances."

Reggie studied every move the parents made, looking for any clue they might be involved in their child's disappearance. So far, they acted the grieving parents, no more.

Twila shook Sage's hand limply, and her voice quivered. "Thank you. We appreciate everything ya 'all are doing to get our baby back."

Hopefully the woman wouldn't break down and not be able to communicate with the press. This conference might enlist sympathy and awareness that could help bring their child home safely. A few tears would work in their favor. Outright blubbering would not.

Reggie led them to stand behind the curtain. "Before you talk with the press, I have a few more questions for you."

The Moores nodded.

"You home school your six-year-old, Blare. Correct." It was admirable, someone was so dedicated to safety and the education of their child that they went to such extreme measures. Not everyone could hack it.

Twila's head rocked up and down. "Yes, we were fortunate enough to swing it. Ryan got a promotion at work while I was pregnant. The extra income allowed me to leave my teaching career to be a full-time mother. So, we decided I should home-school Blare at least until she's in the fifth grade."

Reggie kept her face expressionless. "What was she doing at that time? Shouldn't she be inside doing schoolwork?"

Twila winced. "Blare had a dentist appointment at eleven-thirty. She was nervous. I brought her out to play with her dolls until we had to leave, so it would take her mind off it."

Reggie's tone was even as she spoke. "Tell us again why you left her alone."

Twila emitted a frustrated sigh and gritted her teeth—appearing to be a show of regret. "I was watching her play, sitting on the steps. I'd forgotten to bring my phone out. It rang, and I was afraid the dentist might be canceling. I went inside to answer and told her I'd be right back to stay in there. She never left the yard, and she knew better than to talk to strangers."

Ryan squeezed his wife, still holding her in an embrace. "Blare is a good, obedient child. She'd never leave the yard alone without permission."

"I was only inside about five minutes." The exasperated looking mother appeared ready to burst into tears. Best back off the line of questioning.

"Tell me about the call." Reggie did her best to read the couple. As a trained profiler, Reggie was an expert at it and often got more out of a suspect's reactions than she did their words. Parents were always the first suspects in a child's disappearance, especially one when no ransom call came in. Not that this family could pay, if one had been demanded.

The Moore family wasn't wealthy, though Ryan made a moderate income. They had no source to secure a hefty payoff, should a call come in—unless the kidnapper was after something else. It was a stretch, but Reggie's process was to be thorough. She needed to investigate Ryan Moore's employer and his position to determine if there might be something there the napper was after.

"It was a sales call—a mistake." Twila frowned.

"Mistake?" Reggie probed. Something about this didn't ring true, but she couldn't place exactly what. Was the woman lying?

"Yes. A carpet cleaning company called to confirm their appointment later that day. They wanted to know if there was anything pertinent, they should know before showing up. The thing was, I hadn't made an appointment with them."

"Do you think it was a ruse?" Sage asked.

"Who knows?" Twila shrugged. "The woman calling said I had made an appointment on their online website to have three rooms of carpet cleaned that afternoon. I figured they were just using that line, trying to get an appointment. I wasn't interested. I clean my own carpets."

Magnolia Blossoms

"Or it could've been a typing mistake. Maybe a neighbor had scheduled them and put the address in wrong." Sage suggested.

It was all being checked. Reggie would get to the bottom of the sales call.

"It's time. Ready? Remember, we're not here to answer questions from the press. The sole mission today is to make a plea to whoever took your daughter. Let them know you want Blare back. Ask them to return her safely. They could simply drop her off at home, the fire station, the hospital, or the sheriff's office. Just bring her in. No questions asked."

It was an unlikely scenario at best, but it put options in front of a kidnapper who my regret their actions. If they wanted to back out, Reggie wanted them to know there were ways to return the girl without arrest. At least, they might think so; but she'd be hot on their trail either way.

"Soon as you both plead your case, I'll interrupt and tell the press we're not taking questions." Reggie touched the father's back. He didn't flinch and showed no signs of being extremely nervous—none she could pick up on.

"Here we go." Sage lifted the curtain, and the group gathered behind the podium. Reggie introduced herself, Sage and the Moores. Then she stepped back, as the Moores moved to the microphone. Reggie and Sage flanked the parents.

Their speech was shaky, filled with emotion; but they kept it simple and to-the-point. As their talk ended, reporters began twisting in anticipation of a Q&A.

Reggie gestured for the Moores to move back. Sage took their arms and ushered them behind the curtain.

Reggie stepped to the podium and took the mic. "Ladies and gentlemen, thank you for coming today. Please air the Moore's request as often as you can. Your help in recovering six-year-old Blare Moore is greatly appreciated."

A young woman in the crowd shouted, "What's the status of the investigation?"

"Tell us more," another reporter bellowed.

Reggie put a hand up. "That's all for now. The investigation is ongoing. I have nothing further to report at this time. The press will be alerted with updates as we work to bring Blare Moore safely home. Thank you for your time and attention to this urgent matter." She released the mic and followed Sage and the Moores behind the drape.

"How do you think it went?" Ryan asked, still supporting his wife with an arm.

"Good, it should make an impact." Reggie smiled more confidently than she felt.

Hopefully. They'd thoroughly searched the neighborhood around the Moore home and woodlands withing hiking distance. No sign had been discovered indicating the child had simply wandered off. It was clear, Blare had been abducted. Why was not so clear.

"Go home. Try to relax. Stay near the phone. We've got wire taps on both your lines. It's been a week with no word from the kidnappers. It's unlikely a ransom call will come in this late; . . . but if it does, keep the caller talking if possible. Ask to speak to Blare or see her via video chat, to confirm she's okay. We'll be listening. The agent assigned to you is waiting in the car and will stay with you at your house until this case is resolved."

Ryan's brows furrowed. "By resolved, you mean Blare is returned safely. Right?"

Clearly, they were aware time was running out. Their daughter had been missing for seven days. Whoever took her had made no contact. A grid search had ruled out the possibility of her simply wandering away. They'd talked with the Moore's neighbors within a two-block area. No one had seen or heard anything strange or knew where Blare had disappeared to.

Magnolia Blossoms

Sage and Reggie spoke together. "Absolutely."

Ryan and Twila exited the rear door of the courthouse, shoulders slumped, heads down.

Sage's hand gripped her stomach as she grimaced. "I feel awful for them. I'd be at my wit's end if Ty was missing."

Reggie's head tilted back as she eyed Sage's gesture. "Yeah, what's this?" She patted Sage's hand. Laboring long days at her organic farm, Parsley-Sage-Rose-Mary and Wine, had kept her slim, after giving birth to her and Wyatt's only son four years back.

Ty's birth had delighted the family, since Sage had given up the idea of becoming a mother when her first husband had died. She'd never suspected her move to rural Kentucky would provide her a family of four, with Wyatt and his daughter from his first marriage.

Sage gave her a wide grin. "I haven't told anyone yet but Wyatt. I'm pregnant again—barely, . . . only a couple months; but it's confirmed."

Reggie finally found her smile, and it was a broad one. "Damn, woman, you can't keep such a thing secret. I know you like a book I've read a million times. Shit, I'm so happy for you I could scream."

"That would stir up those reporters." Sage nodded toward the curtain. "A scream might help release some pent-up anxiety. This is a tough case. There's not much to go on yet. We could go to my farm and scream our heads off, like we used to do."

"Yeah, I know. You're a big fan of scream therapy to relieve tension. I might take you up on it if I don't hit a break soon. I'm used to the tension. It never gets easy. Shea helps me work off the stress kinks." Reggie winked and squeezed her best bud.

Sage snickered. "I'll bet he does. Mr. Straight-Laced has done a total turnabout since he met the likes of you. He had no idea who he was messing with when he fell in love with the wackiest female on the planet. That boy flipped head over heels the second he saw you. So is all this sexual therapy of Shea's getting anywhere near getting my best buddy pregnant. It would be awesome for your child to grow up with mine."

"We're certainly enjoying trying, but no foal in the oven yet." Reggie winked then bit her lower lip. "Thanks for helping today. It's tough dealing with parents in this type of situation. They need hope to hang onto. I want them to stay as calm as possible."

Her phone rang. "It's Shea. Can we tell him?" She eyed Sage's tummy.

Sage nodded. "Sure, if Wyatt hasn't already; but we're not spreading it around yet. I want to wait a couple more weeks before we go wide with the news."

"Hey, Babe, did you get a deer?" Reggie smiled to herself, happy to hear her sexy husband's voice.

"Yeah; but, Reggie, . . . we need you and Sage at the farm. Now." Urgency in his voice made hairs stand up on her neck.

Magnolia Blossoms

CHAPTER 2

U. S. Marshal Shea Montgomery stalked through the brush, following the blood trail. His rifle hung from his shoulder, and he held the butt with a hand. His senses were keen, listening for any sign his prey might jump and run again.

It had taken every bit of his well-practiced patience to sit still the twenty minutes he'd deemed for his kill to give out and drop. Moving aside broken branches, he stealthy made his way to a clearing. Water glistened on a lovely pond in sunlight beginning to stream over the water on the pond in the horizon. Dew had settled heavily as dawn approached, and thick grass was wet beneath his waterproof boots. Camo attire and a bright, orange vest kept the cold from his bones, but chilly, autumn, morning air filtered into his lungs. Fragrance of damp foliage and rotting vegetation mixed with heavy pine scent.

There he lay. The monster buck he'd sighted and fired on had flipped and hit the ground with a thud. Then he'd jumped to his feet and sprinted off as though in tip-top condition. *Flight instinct*. The beautiful animal had finally met his expiration beside the still water.

He was motionless, but Shea knew to approach him warily. The primal survival nature of the spectacular breed was strong. One couldn't be too careful. The impressive specimen could fool a man and might still have a last run left in him.

It was part of what made deer hunting a thrill and caused hunters to respect the keen adversary they tracked. No one cared more for the animal population than hunters. Hunting was important for survival of the species. With the human element having taken over most of their wilderness for progress, keeping herds controlled was vital. Otherwise, there wouldn't be enough food to sustain the wild creatures. Sickness would prevail, and the species would genetically weaken over time and eventually become extinct. Hunting licensing fees went to protecting wildlife, to keep not only the sport, but the animals themselves in healthy status.

Shea quietly knelt to check. The buck had expired. Shea laid his weapon on the grass and pulled out his hunting knife and sleeve covers. He worked swiftly, gutting the animal. Getting that done in a timely manner was imperative to ensure the meat didn't have a gamey flavor. He and Reggie enjoyed venison, and it had become a rare treat for them since moving to Salt Lake City.

He was happy being back in Sweetwater. They missed their friends and the quiet pace of rural Kentucky horse country. Salt Lake was supposed to be an interim assignment for him after he'd completed therapy from being shot a couple years back. Reggie had taken the Salt Lake Post a week after their Sweetwater house had burned to the ground. The fiasco that had turned their newlywed lives upside down due to their last Kentucky case.

They'd had a memorable wedding. No one from the Tri-State area would ever forget it. Shea's and Reggie's photos were plastered on every television screen, internet site and newspaper in the country.

Their jobs in Kentucky had depended on their operating under the radar. Those up line had immediately reassigned them, though Shea was out of commission until he healed. The objective was to eventually move back to Sweetwater—after the media died down and folks forgot their faces. Two years later, they were ready to move back, but their posts had been filled by other people in the interim. They needed to find roles in or around town, not an easy thing given their specialties and roles—Reggie's with the FBI and his with the U. S. Marshal's Office.

When he finished, Shea knelt by the waterside and washed his hand and knife. He threw the entrails near the wood line for animals to feed on then pulled his phone out. It was okay to call Wyatt. A phone ringing wouldn't disturb Wyatt's hunt. The Sheriff had fired earlier than Shea had, from his position along the rutted trail that had once served as a farm access road. Surely, he'd tracked and prepared his catch by now.

The base tenor of his tall, broad friend came on the phone. "Find your deer?"

"Yep." Shea snickered. "Big buck. You?"

"Yeah, nice one. I've got him loaded on the quad. Where you at? I'll come pick you up."

"Drive to where you left me. I went up the hell to the tree stand on the right side. I tracked him straight across the drive down a thin trail into a clearing. You can't miss it. Blood trail is evident."

"Gotcha. Be right there."

Shea hung up and stretched his back, tight from sitting still for so long, in order not to scare away potential deer. He took in his surroundings.

Beautiful.

The large clearing would make a picturesque site for a home with enough room for a small coral and nice-sized barn. Reggie would love it.

Something strange appeared in the distance. At first, he couldn't put a finger on it. Then it registered. A large magnolia tree stood in front of the farthest tree line. They didn't grow naturally in the area. It had been purposely planted. He stalked off toward the tree, carrying his weapon.

Wyatt's all-terrain vehicle roared in the distance, growing closer. Shea didn't worry. Wyatt would spot the deer and stopin the clearing.

The thick leaved tree was tall, full and healthy, though at this time of year blossoms were dormant. Grass was thick and lush in front of it, but the ground had sunk a couple inches. Something was buried there.

Be a pet--please. Shea shook his head as he prayed.

Wyatt parked beside Shea's buck. The big man climbed off his rig and tied a rope to Shea's catch, then used the winch on the four-wheeler to drag the hefty animal onto racks attached to the hood. Wyatt's deer lay strapped atop rear racks. Once he secured the buck, he climbed back on the seat and drove to where Shea waited.

"Hey, partner, what gives?" Wyatt grinned, climbing off to stand beside Shea.

Shea nodded toward the patch of sunken ground. "Grave; hope it's not human."

Wyatt rubbed silver stubs beginning to probe through his tanned, square jaw. "By the size of it, it's a big critter or we're out of luck."

"My thinking exactly." Shea groaned as he pulled their folding pack shovel from its binding beside Wyatt's deer. He walked to the gravesite, followed by Wyatt with his own shove. The men begun carefully digging at one corner.

CHAPTER 3

Sage turned off the main road onto the dirt drive into the farm she and Wyatt wanted to purchase. Heirs had neglected the property for over thirty years. They were spread across the world, but the executor confirmed they were open for an offer.

Reggie and Shea agreed to view it while on this rare hunting trip, in hopes it would be suitable for them to purchase together and spilt between them. Reggie had reservations since it could be years before she and Shea could maneuver back to living in or around Sweetwater. It was difficult enough for one of them to get a local assignment, let alone both.

Her concern had wilted a tad. Their visit had turned into a working assignment for Reggie. Eddie Carlson, who'd taken up her previous role on the Human Trafficking Task Force, had been pulled into an undercover assignment.

Her boss, Ben Franks, asked Reggie to assume the post, replacing him temporarily, given the missing child case. "No damned way we can assure how long Carlson will be away," Ben had grumbled in that deep, smoker's voice. She pictured him sitting at his olive-green, military-style, metal desk; feet on the desktop, chair rocked back, and a cigar in one hand.

Magnolia Blossoms

How could she refuse? It was a six-year-old—someone's baby girl. No matter how often she worked cases like this, they broke her heart. Maybe more so as she aged. She and Shea wanted kids so badly she could taste bittersweetness of holding their infant in her arms. The bitter part came from growing dread they might've waited too long to find each other. Her eggs were aging fast at thirty-nine. *Had they turned to dust?*

Sage parked the truck with its door magnet sign reading Parsley-Sage-Rose-Mary-Wine Organic Farm, beside Wyatt's at the edge of a small field off the road. His had a similar sign designating it Sweetwater Sheriff's Department.

The women jumped out of the truck. Sage unhinged the trailer from the hitch. Reggie dropped the ramp then climbed inside the Gator® they'd borrowed from Sage's farm. She backed it off the trailer and onto the rugged driveway. Sage climbed back into the truck and pulled it away from the trailer and back onto the drive.

A roar of a four-wheeler sounded, as Wyatt cleared the tree line and stopped behind Sage's vehicle. She walked over and flipped the tailgate down. Reggie parked the Gator and went to help the couple. The threesome hefted the heavy deer off the front and back of Wyatt's quad, slid them into the truck bed, and Sage shut the tailgate.

"Thanks for coming so quickly. Who knew our hunting trip would turn into a murder investigation?" The tall, handsome sheriff winced, slipping an arm around his wife and using his other to wave toward Reggie.

"No problem, babe." Sage snuggled beneath her giant husband's bulky arm and wrapped her arm around his slim waist. "I'm always eager for a chance to see my man." Her face turned upward, love glowing from her dark eyes.

He bent to give her a tender kiss that lasted so long it brought tinges of unnecessary jealousy, to Reggie. She was about to see the man of her dreams, the one she shared her life with, the one she'd nearly given up on finding. Reggie was the luckiest woman on earth to have finally stumbled on the one man who appreciated her devotion to her career, her wacky sense of humor and crazy wit. They'd known each other only five years, but in that time nearly lost each other more than once. Each day together was a blessing she'd never ignore.

When the love birds broke up, Wyatt patted his wife's slim behind. "Thanks for taking the deer to the check station for us. Be sure to go straight to the meat processing plant. It's important the meat get cooled down soon as possible.

"Not a problem. I'm on it, boss." She saluted Wyatt then jumped up and gave him a last peck on the lips before waltzing to her truck and pulling away. Sage drove slowly down the lane to the highway, and as she pulled out, another Sheriff's truck pulled in.

"We're going to need your expertise in profiling on this one, Reggie. It appears a simple murder, so it's staying my case. You've got enough to do with our child abduction."

"Not a problem, Wyatt, whatever you need. It's a shame the grid search and neighboring interviews turned up nothing. It appears a kidnapping. The press conference went well today, though time is running out. There's still no ransom request, and I doubt there will be. The family has no means to pay a hefty ransom, from what we've learned so far."

Deputy Leo Sanders parked his truck where Sage had vacated. He and his partner Jaiden Coldwater hopped from the truck and came to stand with Wyatt and Reggie.

"Good to see you," Leo shook Reggie's hand.

"Same here, Leo; unfortunately, it's not at a table over a beer.

Jaiden threw her arms around her friend. "We'll get there eventually once the dirty work is done. We've missed you, gal."

Reggie hugged her back. "Same here. Shea and I are doing everything we can to move back here."

"This is some vacation you're having." Leo snickered.

Reggie shrugged. "Comes with the job. Crime is everywhere. Got to do what you've got to do."

"You've got that right, sister. We're lucky you were in town soon after the girl disappeared." Jaiden stood spread legged, hands-on utility belt, her full five-foot-one frame held still.

The tiny imp was an impressive law woman, with years of experience as a Texas Ranger. By chance she'd come to live in Sweetwater when Wyatt needed to replace a deputy. She'd proven herself a fierce adversary to crime, and Reggie had learned not underestimate the pint-sized deputy.

Leo, on the other hand, had spent his fifteen years working on the Sheriff's force. The pair was Wyatt's top, most experienced team. He might look like a grown-up Opie Taylor, with blonde hair and thick shoulders; but he was a keen, knowledgeable lawman and sharpshooter.

"What have we got?" He studied Wyatt.

"You'll soon see. Body, probably female. Strange one. Good, here comes the coroner. Between Reggie's profiling and Baker's forensics, we'll soon know more."

The deputies strode to their truck and drove their quads off the trailer, as Baker's four-seater truck pulled to a stop beside them. He too, pulled a trailer with off-the-road equipment. Two uniform men wearing navy blue coveralls stepped from the passenger side. Coroner Sam Baker hopped down from the driver's side.

His short stature and thick frame were covered with the same uniform as his men, only his was white. Combed-over wisps of greying hair floated up in the early morning breeze. He slapped them down Thick glasses sat prominently on his round face atop the few wrinkles that had settled around his clear, blue eyes.

With waves at the group of law people waiting, the threesome set about disembarking their off-the-road vehicles from the trailer they'd towed. Two quads and a four-seater rover carrying the coroner's men lined behind those waiting.

"Let's get at it," Baker gestured to the rutted trail, surprisingly without his usual joking banter. The man took every opportunity to try out new jokes. You'd think he was practicing for a standup comedy routine. It was part of his charm and since he was the top forensics expert in the state, everyone indulged his silly quirk.

Wyatt climbed onto his quad, as did Leo and Jaiden. Reggie started the Gator, and the procession followed the Sheriff. Thick woods flanked the farm lane. Tall pines of different variations, healthy walnut trees, gigantic oaks, elms and the occasional dogwood or pawpaw tree, had spattered among lofty firs.

About a mile along, Wyatt turned off the dirt lane onto a narrow trail where thick grass had been worn by animals. The sun was midway to noon. It must be around ten o'clock. Dew lay thick on branches slapping the vehicle as she drove behind her best male bud—besides Shea. Land lay flat to gently rolling as they exited the trees into an enormous clearing, probably around twenty acres or more, surrounded by woods. To the far side a tree-covered mountain appeared to guard the lovely space. What looked to be a two-acre lake, sat close by.

Shea's orange vest and hat caught her eye in the distance. She'd never have seen him in his camo attire, had he not worn the protective gear. He waved, having noticed their arrival. She followed Wyatt with the rest of their group, across the field to her man.

Magnolia Blossoms

With waves at the group of law people waiting, the threesome set about disembarking their off-the-road vehicles from the trailer they'd towed. Two quads and a four-seater rover lined behind those waiting.

"Let's get at it," Baker gestured to the rutted trail, surprisingly without his usual joking banter. The man took every opportunity to try out new jokes. You'd think he was practicing for a standup comedy routine. It was part of his charm and since he was the top forensics expert in the state, everyone indulged his silly quirk.

Wyatt climbed onto his quad, as did Leo and Jaiden. Reggie started the Gator, and the procession followed the Sheriff. Thick woods flanked the farm lane. Tall pines of different variations, healthy walnut trees, gigantic oaks, elms and the occasional dogwood or pawpaw tree, had spattered among lofty firs.

About a mile along, Wyatt turned off the dirt lane onto a narrow trail where animals had worn thick grass. The sun was midway to noon. It must be around ten o'clock. Dew lay thick on branches slapping the vehicle as she drove behind her best male bud—besides Shea. Land lay flat to gently rolling as they exited the trees into an enormous clearing, around twenty acres or more, surrounded by woods. To the far side a tree-covered mountain guarded the lovely space. What looked to be a two-acre lake, sat close by.

Shea's orange vest and hat caught her eye in the distance. She'd never have seen him in his camo attire, had he not worn the protective gear. He waved, having noticed their arrival. She followed Wyatt with the rest of their group, across the field to her man.

Magnolia Blossoms

CHAPTER 4

Dismounting, new arrivals went about their individual tasks. Leo and Jaiden pulled out gear to secure the crime scene. Baker and his men brought a body bag and shovels to continue excavation of the body.

"Hey, babe; thanks for coming." Shea took her in his arms. Her head rested against his chest.

"Nice hunting trip, Shea." Reggie squeezed him and gave him a half-hearted smile.

His lips twisted sideways. "You and I have a knack for digging up danger."

She slapped his firm buttocks. "Funny man, you taking over Baker's role as sarcastic comedian with a death twist?"

"Hell." He released her, and they pulled out protective gear from the Gator. "If you can't laugh at crazy shit, the job will turn you into a sour, shriveled pumpkin."

She snickered and winked. "Yeah, I like it. You don't shrivel quickly, and you're learning to like crazy shit."

"I married you, didn't I?" He grinned, the sexy way that made her insides bubble like a carbonated soda, then bent to slip covers over his boots.

"Lucky you." She winked back, slipping gloves onto her hands.

"Ready." He looked her up and down. Twinkle in his eyes showed he wasn't asking about her crime-scene attire.

"You know me, babe. I'm always ready." She stood on tiptoes and accepted the peck on her lips. "Let's get to it." Turning, she strode toward the gravesite, his footfalls on thick grass behind her.

Shea had dug up only enough of the shallow grave to confirm it was not animal remains. Baker's men were carefully exhuming the body. Wyatt and his team were walking a grid search around the discover site.

Surveying the area, she chewed the side of her upper lip. "Beautiful place for a burial." Her head tilted. "Wyatt, magnolia trees don't grow naturally in this area. Do they?"

The giant of a man stood and stretched. "Nope, they're more of a southern native. We're all hardwoods, firs and pines in Kentucky."

"So, someone planted this tree. Wonder if it was when the victim was buried or planted before for some reason. Strange to plant it at random out here in the middle of nowhere."

Shea pointed to it. "It's a tall, mature tree. Depending on how big it was when planted, I'd say it's maybe fifteen-to-twenty years old."

Reggie nodded. "Learned a thing or two growing up in Florida I see."

Shea gave her a sarcastic grin. "That I never want to live there, yes. I have always had an interest in trees. Besides Florida, I was stationed in Georgia for a while."

The two of them had lived all over, moving from assignment to assignment. They had decided they wanted to make their home in Sweetwater, Kentucky.

Reggie, Wyatt and other friends had grown up there. Her parents had dumped her on her grandparents, when she reached school age, so she'd get a decent education. Before that, they'd dragged her across the globe, working in one desolate place after another, taking care of other individuals' children through Doctors Without Borders. Giving her up was the best thing they could've done for Reggie. Not only had she gotten stability of her loving grandparents. She'd met people who remained vital parts of her life to this day—Wyatt among them.

Sam stood and stretched, as his men unearthed the final parts of the corpse wrapped in a floral printed cotton piece of fabric. The only part that had been visible from Shea's digging, had been a set of white-sock clad feet, a size six or seven. Now it was clear. The socks were trimmed with white lace, like a small child might wear.

Reggie pulled out a recording device. She talked into it explaining who was there and what they were doing. "White socks trimmed in white lace are more like something a small child would wear. Odd for someone with a size six or seven sized foot, wouldn't you say, Sam?"

"I'd estimate the size about a six." He nodded.

Reggie held the recorder to her lips. "Clearly whoever buried the victim wanted to cover the evidence, covering their shame for their part in it, by wrapping her in the pretty cloth. They must've cared for the victim."

Sam knelt beside the body. He unfolded the cloth aside, laying the edges gently on the ground to the sides of the body, as it extended beneath it.

Reggie began reciting into her recording device. "Coroner Baker has lifted the covering fabric. The skeleton is of a small female. Long, brown hair has been tied to each side in ponytails. Eyes closed."

Sam leaned toward Reggie to be heard. "With no coffin or embalming, the body in the ground is exposed to nature quicker. In such conditions, total decomposition takes eight-to-ten years. Cartilage, bones and hair stay intact much longer than muscles and organs. Decay of this body shows it has been in the ground for at least ten years, possibly a bit longer. I need to assess bone structure to give a more precise time of burial."

"Shit," Jaiden spat. "A child killer has been on the loose in Sweetwater for ten years or more"

Leo squeezed his eyes shut. "Right under our noses."

"We're going to catch this son-of-a-bitch." Wyatt slid a broad hand through his silky, silver locks, then plopped his hunting hat back atop them.

Reggie pursed her lips a second while she bit down anger that rose in situations like this. It never got easier when motherfuckers killed kids. Putting her professional persona in charge, she pulled the mic to her lips. "Girl is wearing a childish style dress with a round, white color constructed of a pink floral in what appears to be cotton. No hosiery other than the socks. No shoes. No jewelry, nail polish or other adornments. No visible tattoos. No sigh of abuse visible, but with skin disuse decayed, trauma must be determined during autopsy from examination of bones. Pink ribbons tied around pigtails of long, brown hair. It appears the magnolia tree nearby is a marker for the grave, but that is uncertain at this point. It appears to have been planted somewhere near the approximate assumed burial time." She clicked the machine off.

The aides folded the covering over the child's body, then eased it into the black bag and zipped it shut. They lifted the child, careful not to damage remains, and carried it to the coroner's vehicle. The deputies went back to their stopping point, walking the grid to look for clues. Given the extended time since burial, it was unlikely they'd find anything more.

Sam shook Reggie, Shea's and Wyatt's hands. "You all come in tomorrow. I'll have a report for you." To his crew he yelled. "I need this whole plat of earth brought in. You know the drill."

Reggie shook her head. "This is Wyatt's case."

Wyatt gave her a knowing look, getting she didn't want to step on his toes; and Shea was technically a civilian on vacation. "No problem. If you and Shea don't mind, I'd like a couple extra expert eyes on this. Reggie, I won't pull you too much off the abduction. It's your priority, but if there's a kid killer out there for over a decade, I need all the advice I can get."

"Sure, buddy; we'd do anything to help you out." Shea patted their friend on his sturdy back. "We'll meet you at Sam's office. Is nine okay?"

Wyatt nodded agreement. "Yeah, thanks."

Magnolia Blossoms

CHAPTER 5

True to their word, Shea and Reggie were waiting at Coroner Sam Baker's office when Wyatt rolled in at nine a.m. the next day. Wyatt took a last swig of his coffee and dropped his cup into a receptacle by the door. "Morning, ya' all."

"Howdy yourself." Reggie snickered glad she'd opted for breakfast later. Dissected bodies and a full stomach didn't agree with her, even after all her years on the job.

Shea shook the hand Wyatt extended. "Let's get this over with." Her loving hubby didn't enjoy this part of the work any better than Reggie did.

"Before we go in let me fill you in. CSI has been combing the farm where we found that child. They've discovered and brought in two other bodies. Each of them was wrapped and dressed in a similar fashion to the one we found. They appeared to have been buried similar to our girl. Each had a magnolia tree planted beside it—the only one nearby. One was younger than the other two. The other was the older."

Reggie rolled eyes heavenward and spun, hands clenched at her side. "Son of a bitch."

"Damn it to hell, Wyatt, there's a serial killer in the area." Shea's fist pounded the wall he'd been leaning against.

"Exactly. Reggie, this makes it an FBI case, but so is the child abduction. Your call on this." Wyatt gritted teeth together emitting a sigh through them.

She shook her head. "Wyatt, you know I'm only here to fill in. This isn't my regular assignment. I just happened to be here at a convenient time, when the kid went missing, to take over for Eddie Carlson, when he got pulled into an undercover operation. My boss, Ben Franks, said Carlson shouldn't be long, but wanted me to take over. I can bring in more agents to help with investigation and I'll happily work on this one with you, but I'm going to need you and your staff to continue working hand-in-hand with my team. You all know this place better than anyone."

Wyatt acted relieved. "I was hoping you'd say that. We've worked well together in the past. No reason to do it differently now. What about you, Shea? You're here on vacation, but with children as victims of this crime, the U. S. Marshal's Office should be involved."

Shea bit the side of his lower lip. "Yeah, how about I call my upline, Darin Spenser. He'll want first notice and will probably assign Andy Davis, the Marshal who took my post here when I was reassigned to Salt Lake City."

"Yeah, and I need to call Ben. Maybe he can pull Carlson off undercover to get him back on the job here." She felt like she was stepping on Carlson's toes, though her taking over work on the missing girl hadn't been her choice. She'd just been in the right place at the right time. Or was it the wrong place at the wrong time.

This sure as hell wasn't the vacation she and Shea had anticipated. They'd come to Sweetwater to view a plat of property; to spend time with friends like Wyatt and Sage;

and so, Shea and Wyatt could finally go deer hunting together.

"Why don't the two of you go ahead and call before we see Sam. I've got a couple calls to make as well."

Wyatt walked further down the empty, sterile hallway in the basement of the hospital. Reggie and Shea exited the outside double doors and split, one heading left, the other right. Her mouth watered at the rear view of her handsome, lanky husband. Sexy as hell, having bulked up his arms and shoulders. His lean waist and slim legs set off the most droolworthy butt she'd ever seen. She thanked God every day for Shea by her side. Otherwise, she'd have nothing but bad guys and dead people in her life. She hit send on Ben's number.

"Franks here. What's up? Find that kid?" The familiar, gruff voice growled.

"On the trail, but nothing significant yet. You know the girl Shea and Wyatt discovered?"

"Yeah, you ID her?"

"Not yet, but there's another development in that case. It appears there's a serial killer on the loose. One who has been working the area for many years. A couple other children have been discovered on the same farm."

"Son of a bitch!" She could see him spinning in his nearly-worn-out office chair.

"Yeah, and there's no way I can find the missing girl and catch a decade's old serial killer case. I need you to send in some help. When can you bring Carlson back to his post? I've got another job . . . in Salt Lake City."

"Awh, shit, I was meaning to talk with you about that. I was hoping to wait until you found that kid first. It appears Eddie Carlson is going to have to stay undercover considerably longer than we had estimated. The Sweetwater post is the US Midwest center for focus on missing and abducted children. It is conveniently located for trafficking the I75, I71, I64 corridor and has easy access to airfare, with proximity to Cincinnati, Indianapolis, Lexington, Dayton, Memphis, Nashville and St. Louis airports. I need someone on that post with venom in their eyes when it comes to abused and abducted children. I know how you feel about that. You're wasted in Salt Lake. I want you back in your old post in Sweetwater. I can put someone else in Utah. What do you think?"

"You know I've wanted to get back to somewhere near Sweetwater ever since I lost this post. What about the media?" Was it too good to be true? This would be an answered prayer.

"Hell, it's been almost two years since the fiasco. If they haven't forgotten you and Shea by now, they never will. Just say yes and keep a low profile . . . keep your mug out of the press. Capuche?" Franks grumbled.

She pictured him with elbows on his desk. Stubby hands running through the greyed ring of hair left growing around his shiny globe. "I'd love to jump on this, but I've got to consider Shea. I'll talk with him and get back to you."

"Damn it, Casse." Thud of his fist hitting the desktop sounded in her ear.

"It's Montgomery. I'm married. Remember? I can't make a decision like this without talking to Shea."

"Crap. I know. Just do it. Make it happen. In the meantime, get your cute, little ass shaking and find that kid. Take charge of the serial gig and play well with the locals. I'll send in the troops to help. You're in charge." He clicked off.

"Bye to you too." She grinned at the phone, used to his brash manner. Ben adored her and respected her work. She felt the same of him. Their relationship worked perfectly for them both.

She spun toward him as Shea turned to face her, flipping his phone into his belt holder. Worry framed his face.

Clearly his discussion with his boss had been as frustrating as hers. She wiggled her shoulders to release tension, and with snap-crackle-pop her they relaxed. She strode toward her man with a forced smile.

They met at the walkway into the basement floor of the hospital and joining hands, walked silently inside to meet Wyatt. He blew a kiss into his phone, clicked off and slid the cell into its compartment. "How'd it go?"

Reggie glanced at Shea, telling him with her eyes to go first. She was dying to hear what his upline, Darin Spenser, had to say. She had hesitated to ask him outside, not wanting to make him repeat it. He would have to tell Wyatt anyway. Might as well hear it at the same time.

With a rock of his head, Shea looked toward Wyatt then back at her. "Andy Davis, the Marshal who replaced me here in Sweetwater, is from Florida. He'd been undercover for a few years and promised his wife he'd be more accessible from then on. He took this role in Kentucky with the assumption his wife and teenaged son would join him after the boy graduated high school. He's a senior now, playing basketball in anticipation of a scholarship. Moving here with him in school would screw that up. The boy is a handful, and though his wife originally agreed to the arrangement, she has had second thoughts. She wants him around now, to help her finish raising their son. That was not enough to get Andy to request a transfer back to Florida, but his wife had a car accident over the weekend. She's in a cast and banged up, unable to drive for several weeks. He's gone home to Florida to be with his family. Darin doubts Davis will be willing tom return to Kentucky. He asked me to not only help with the current cases, but to consider being transferred back here long term—starting as soon as I'm able to—meaning immediately." His head rocked easily from her to Wyatt and back as he spoke, but he ended his spiel facing his wife with a sheepish grin.

Magnolia Blossoms

She let out a hoot. "Damn, Babe, that's good news. Franks said Carlson is going to be undercover for an extended time. He asked me to take my old post here back . . . starting soon as possible. We've hit the lottery of job assignments." She flung her petite person at her husband's torso as his arms opened instinctively to catch her. Her legs wrapped around his waist; and his hands clutched her buttocks, as she wrapped arms around his shoulders.

"Let's do this thing, woman. What do you say?"

"I say hell yes." She planted hands around his strong jaw and a kiss on his delectable lips, savoring their softness and the taste she had grown addicted to.

"I'll second that motion." Wyatt chuckled behind them. "Now, if you two can pry yourselves apart for a while, we shouldn't keep Doc Baker any longer.

With a final smackeroo on those delicious lips, Reggie hopped down landing her navy pumps softly aground, as Shea released her. She straightened her uniform of choice, a navy pantsuit with a hot pink tank top. Shade of tank was optional but always bright. "Let's do this."

Wyatt pushed the double doors open to Coroner Sam's domain. Chilly air engulfed the threesome as they entered, along with an overwhelming odor of blood and formaldehyde. The elderly, short man wearing a white coat strode forward to greet his visitors with a handout. They shook and braced for the anticipated forthcoming of stale death comedy the coroner was prone to.

"You're here to talk about the girls, right?"

"Sure thing," Wyatt nodded.

"Didn't think you were here to see the guy who was smothered to death by a couple of breasts." To Reggie he winced. "No offense, Agent Casse, I mean Montgomery."

"None taken. I haven't heard about that case." She snickered.

"Yes, the poor guy didn't even struggle."

Shea burst into a laugh. "Can't blame the dude."

So, it was one of his jokes. She allowed him a titter to appease the wacky coroner, always wondering what he had come up with next. Guess it was his way of living with the stress of working on dead people every day.

"A pal of mine's a college professor. The day before he gave the final exam, he warned students the only excuse for missing the following day's exam that would be considered were nuclear attack, serious personal injury, illness or death in the immediate family. A student asked, "What if I'm suffering from complete and utter sexual exhaustion?" My professor friend answered sympathetically, "Well, I guess you'd have to write the exam with your other hand."

After a satisfying round of laughter by his audience, Wyatt patted the back of the aging doctor. "Don't give up your day job, old friend. Now, how about we get to those bodies?"

Doc Baker turned, walked toward the covered lump on the operating table. "I have to say, this is the most interesting case I've seen in a long while. First, let me give you some background.

A decomposing body significantly alters chemistry of soil beneath it, causing changes that may persist for years. That is why I required the dirt around the body be brought to the lab for examination. As the body begins to decompose, purging releases nutrients into the underlying soil. Maggot migration transfers much of the energy in a body to the wider environment. Eventually, the process creates a *'cadaver decomposition island,'* a highly concentrated area of organically rich soil. As well as releasing nutrients into the wider ecosystem, the cadaver also attracts other organic materials, such as dead insects and fecal matter from larger animals. The average human body consists of fifty-to-seventy-five percent chemicals. Every kilogram of dry body mass eventually releases 32g of nitrogen, 10g of phosphorous, 4g of potassium, and 1g of magnesium into the soil. Initially, some underlying and surrounding vegetation dies off, possibly because of nitrogen toxicity, or because of antibiotics in the body secreted by insect larvae that feed on the flesh. This process is beneficial to the ecosystem. Thus, the eventual fertile landmass around the decayed corpse."

"So, trees planted at approximately the same time would be lush and healthy." Shea's comment wasn't a question, only a summary of what he and they were hearing.

Regardless, Doc Baker nodded. "Indeed. These children have been buried for some time." His arm waved toward two other operating tables also holding covered remains. "Enough, in fact, for them to rot to a point where they provided a delightful haven for growing trees, with exception of the latest one. It was evident from soil-based chemicals, this child," he pointed to a fleshy corpse, "had been buried approximately two-to-three weeks."

Shea screwed his lips up. "So, that child was approximately twelve-to-thirteen years old, and she was buried about two-three weeks."

"Exactly." Doc Baker strolled to one of the other tables. "These two were approximately the same age when they died. Fibers in their mouth cavities indicate they all three died of asphyxiation." He flipped the cover back on the third cadaver. "They were all three dressed similar, like younger girls. Their long hair was in pigtails with ribbons. No shoes, but all three wore white socks with lace sewn around the cuffs."

Reggie put a hand to her chin, going into profiler mode. "The killer wanted them to be young, little girls. They were killed because they were getting too big. At twelve or thirteen, they were entering puberty, possibly developing breasts and having menses."

"Exactly my thoughts." Doc Baker nodded returning his gaze to the corpses on his table. "The biggest difference I've found with these victims is the length of time since death and burial. This one," he pointed to one having some dried fleshy fiber left on its bones, "was buried approximately twelve years ago." He turned to the third table. "This girl was buried about eighteen years ago."

Reggie continued to profile. "Six years apart. The killer is selecting pre-teens or early teens, killing them, then dressing them like much younger girls. Wonder if there are more victims to be found. This timeline, the number years and age of the victims is significant. It is meaningful. Somehow. We need to figure out how and why, to catch this bastard."

Shea gripped her hand to his side. "Yes. So is the planting of a magnolia tree to mark the grave."

She sadly smiled up into his gorgeous, green peepers. "He's careful with them. He takes great pains to prepare them for burial. The tree symbolizes something. We need to know what. It's as though he's paying respects and maybe wants to mark the grave so he can come back and visit them. He loves them or fanaticizes he does."

Shea squeezed her hand. "I'll get with Carla Orson at National Center for Missing and Exploited Children, and we'll search for missing girls fitting the report's description at six-year intervals starting now, twelve years ago, eighteen and twenty-four . . . in case this asshole was at it before the oldest body we unearthed."

Wyatt shifted his stance. "A forensic artist has drawn visuals of what the girls might've looked like at the age of demise. It's in the file. I asked CSI to send complete files to you both, as they sent it to me. You should be able to access it now."

"Great." Reggie's fingers rubbed back and forth across Shea's as he held her hand. "We need to be visually aware of any magnolia trees in the area. God knows where the killer buried previous victims, assuming there were any. Anyone with a magnolia tree around is suspect."

"That takes up a lot of folks. Those trees might not be native to Sweetwater, but they're popular, just the same." Seriousness in Wyatt's deep voice made it sound gravelly.

Baker covered the bodies and strolled with them following toward his desk near the exit door. "About fibers in their mouths, CSI is processing DNA now. They will compare it to the victims."

Shea's head rocked up and down. "Good, as we find possible girls from the missing child database, we'll flag those with DNA files and compare them to CSI's findings."

"DNA should be ready in a couple days." Baker leaned his behind on his desk and crossed arms.

"Damn, we've got a lot of work to do." Wyatt shook Baker's hand, as did Shea. Then he led them out the double doors."

"And we've got a little girl to find." Reggie double-stepped trying to keep up with the two tall men walking in front of her.

CHAPTER 6

Reggie took the seat Carlson Bain offered. Shea sat in the one beside her, across from Mr. Bain, Ryan Moore's employer at the toy factory. "Thank you for speaking with us Mr. Bain. As you know, we are investigating the disappearance of your employee, Ryan Moore's daughter, Blare."

"No problem, the thin, blond thirty-something man winced. "Yes, I spoke with Ryan earlier today. He and his wife Twila are at their wit's end with worry."

Shea sat back in his seat. "Yes, and that's why we're here. Anything at all we might learn from you could potentially point us in the right direction to locate Blare Moore."

Tension was evident in Bain's body. "Absolutely, I'm happy to help in any way I can, but I don't see how I might be of service."

Reggie put on her most serious interrogation face, eyeing the gentleman. "The child has been missing for ten days now. There has been no ransom request or strong lead as to her whereabouts."

"Surely you don't suspect me or another of our employees." Bain's eyes squinted.

Magnolia Blossoms

She liked them nervous. "We are covering every possible base to ensure we don't miss anything relevant. Can you tell us about Ryan's position, any access he might have to large sums of cash or other valuable properties or sensitive material?"

Carlson visibly relaxed a tad. "Well, that's simple enough. Ryan is the head of our Customer Service Department. He has no access whatsoever to proprietary information, valuables or cash."

She nodded. "I understand his position is a recent promotion."

Carlson clasped hands in his lap. "Yes, he was promoted from Customer Service Rep about six months ago. The promotion came with a substantial raise."

Shea interjected, "Yes, his wife told it the additional funds allowed her to become a stay-at-home mother and to home school Blare. Can you tell us about Ryan's work and relationships with co-workers?"

Carlson glanced right, as though thinking. "Ryan keeps to himself. I do not believe he socializes with those in his department, never has that I know of. He's quiet, a good worker, dependable and businesslike."

She dove deeper. "Are there any rifts you're aware of between Ryan and his team or other employees?"

Carlson met her gaze. "None I've heard of. Far as I know, he does not socialize or interact with company employees outside his team, with me and with contacts necessary in doing his daily work. He's a good employee."

She stood, having clearly gotten all they could out of Carlson. "Thank you for setting up a conference rooms where Marshal Montgomery and I can speak individually with Ryan's team. Shea will take the two men and I'll meet with the two women."

"Not a problem. Let me know if there's anything else I can do. My secretary will show you out when you've finished here." Carlson stoon and led them to a row of room with doors open. She stepped into one and She took the next one. "I'll send your first interviewees in." He walked away.

Within a couple minutes, a forty-something female with shaggy, bleached blonde locks in need of a redo, strolled into Reggie's compartment.

"Please, shut the door and have a seat." Reggie indicated she should take the chair across the small table. The woman's shoulders hung loosely, and she rolled eyes before doing as instructed. She slumped slightly in the chair and clasped hands together on the table, making it difficult to miss her chipped, red polish. Wrinkled shirt and slacks added to Reggie's impression the woman cared little for her appearance, as did clumpy mascara and lack of other makeup.

Reggie extended a hand, which was met by a limp shake from a sweaty palm. "I'm FBI Special Agent Reggie Montgomery, and I'm here with my associate next door to learn anything we can that might help in our search for your manager, Ryan Moore's, daughter Blare Moore. You are?"

The gal slunk back into her chair. "Betsy Farmer. Listen, I've got no beef with Moore. You're not pinning this on me."

Her defensive manner didn't surprise Reggie. "We're not here to pin anything on anyone. We need to understand what you know about Ryan Moore, his wife Twila, and their daughter Blare."

Betsy straightened. "I know nothing. Moore keeps to himself. He's a loner. Hell, I did not even know the dude had a family. He never talks to no one. He never had photos or personal things on his desk, even when he was one of us."

"Are you aware of any rifts between Mr. Moore and anyone else, or have you ever witnessed any altercation between him and another?"

"Shit, no. I've barely heard him speak to anyone outside of our team, Bain and customers—back when he was a CSR."

"How did you feel about his being promoted?"

Her mouth screwed up, face shifted to the side and back. "I've been here longer than Moore, and I got passed up when they gave that role to him. I ain't saying he doesn't deserve it. But you get my drift. It stings to be screwed over."

"Do you feel Moore screwed you over? How is he to work for?"

Her head shook. "Nah, Moore didn't do the screwing. He is an okay guy, I guess. I barely know him. He stays out of my way, long as I do the work."

"Would you say his treatment of you is fair?" She dove even farther.

Betsy shrugged. "Guess so."

Obviously, this was all Betsy was about to offer. Time to move on. "Thank you, Betsy, can you send in Mrs. Dunson, please?"

Betsy stood and slinked out of the room. Moments later a fifty-something woman entered. Her slim body was wrapped tightly in a sweater cardigan with matching top adorned by a pearl necklace and loose-fitting pleated skirt that hung to between her knees and ankles. Support hose and black, sensible shoes added to her frumpy appearance, as did tight pin curls in her greying black hair. She smiled at Reggie.

"You must be Mrs. Kim Dunson." Reggie extended her hand. "I'm FBI Special Agent Reggie Montgomery."

Rail-thin, gnarly fingers with unpolished nails grasped it in a hardy shake. "Yes, pleased to meet you." The other hand shoved the door shut.

"Please have a seat." Reggie folded hands atop the table. "As you might've gathered my associate and I are here investigating the disappearance of Blare Moore, your manager, Ryan Moore's daughter."

"Yes, I've heard. I feel so sorry for that poor boy. He is such a nice man. Never butts in where his nose should not be. He is easy to work for. If there is anything at all I can do to help find that baby, please tell me. I have grandchildren about her age."

"Yes, please, tell me anything you've noticed out of the ordinary about Ryan Moore. Are you aware of anyone who might have issue with him? Is there anyone he's had words with? How does he get along with people in the office?"

"He's a quiet one, not a bad thing. He never argued with customers when he was a CSR. He was a good worker and deserved the promotion. I guess he gets along with everyone else well. I stay out of people's business, you know. Only thing I can think of is Betsy seemed to resent his promotion. Probably thought it should have gone to her, but that poor girl has had a hard time the last few years. She might have been running around and hit the meds a bit too much for a while there. She was notoriously late for work when she was hell-bent for leather trying to get past the pain of divorce. I reckon that is why she got passed over and they gave it to Ryan. He was deserving—more than Betsy."

"I see. Have you witnessed or heard of any argument between them about it or anything else?"

Her hands went to the table. "Oh, no, dear. I did not mean to imply Betsy has something to do with that baby's disappearance. It is just that she's the only person who even seems to have taken notice of Ryan Moore. He is one of those fellas who blends into the woodwork. You know the type?"

Reggie nodded, disappointed but happy at the same time. "Well, if there's anything else you think of, please contact me." She stood, and the older woman did the same.

"Will do. Find that girl, now. You hear?" With that, she walked out, leaving the door wide.

Moments later, a man exited Shea's meeting room. Her husband walked out behind him, turning to her. "Done here?"

She linked arms with him and tugged him toward the receptionist desk, where Bain's secretary worked. "Yep."

Once they turned badges in and left the building, she smiled up into those emerald eyes. "Learn anything?"

"Not a freaking thing that might help. How about you?" Shea opened the passenger side door for her.

She slid in. "Not much, only that one of the women had worked here longer and resented Ryan getting promoted over her. The other gal informed me of why she things it happened. Apparently, Betsy Farmer screwed up her chance by frequently being late to work. Her appearance sure doesn't fit someone trying for a potential promotion. She's kind of a mess."

He shut the door and rounded the truck, climbing behind the wheel. "Think she's involved?"

"Not really. She acts way too lazy to be involved in a kidnapping,"

"Another dead end." He started the engine.

"Afraid so." Time was passing quickly. No leads. Parents are frantic and do not appear to be the culprits. It was growing increasingly likely they would find Blare Farmer dead . . . if at all.

CHAPTER 7

Reggie, Wyatt and Shea combed the area, knocking on doors of neighbors once again, interviewing everyone they could find at home. Deputies Jaiden Coldwater and Leo Sanders took outlying streets and did the same. This time they investigated in the evening, so were luckier than during earlier rounds. The three law enforcement officers split up.

Reggie knocked on a neighbor's door. A lady appearing to be in her late thirties answered, a toddler on one hip and a dishrag in another. Dishwater brown hair escaping a bun floated in the air around her face like a smoky halo. Bright, friendly eyes greeted Reggie, though the woman was clearly busy. "Can I help you?"

She flicked her badge open. "I'm hoping so." Reggie introduced herself. "You are?"

"Carol Lang."

"Ms. Lang, we're canvassing the neighborhood again trying to learn any tiny tidbit of information that might help us locate the missing child in your neighborhood."

The woman let out a sigh with a sad smile on her face and a glance at her baby. "Yeah, we will all feel more relieved when you find her or catch whoever has taken that child. I'm terrified to let mine out of eyesight.

"Where were you the day Blare Moore disappeared? Did you notice anything strange that day? Have you seen or heard anything suspicious?" Reggie stowed her badge and flipped out her phone to take notes.

"Honestly, hon, I was shopping that day. Tough to do with this one and a four-year-old along, but we've got to eat. By the time I got home, there were police cars all over the place and they had the street blocked off. I spoke to that nice Native American Deputy. Jaiden, I believe is her name. I'd love to find whatever bastard took that baby and get him alone for a few minutes. If you know what I mean. I have zilch that might help. But I belong to the church on the next block. I'm a devout Christian. I've been praying for that little girl."

Reggie glanced around the yard and her eye caught something. "I see you have a couple magnolia trees in your back yard. Do you like them? Some say they have special significance."

Ms. Lang shrugged. "They're fine, I guess. No trouble, and when they bloom the blossoms are lovely. Leaves are nice and shiny all the time. Not sure about significance. They were here when we bought the place."

"You and your husband wouldn't happen to have all-terrain vehicle, would you?"

Carol's brow furrowed. "You mean like a Jeep?"

"No, more like a four-wheeler, a quad, something you can take on trails where a car won't go."

Carol smiled as her chin rose. "Heavens no. Mike and I aren't the woodsy types. He considers roughing it when we stay in anything but a four-star hotel. Besides, these little ones are a handful. We rarely have time away from them to visit museums and historic sites. That's more our speed."

"Gotcha. Thanks for your time." Reggie flipped her a card, which she took. "Call me, day or night, if you think of anything that might help.

As the woman stuffed the card in her shorts pocket and closed the door, Reggie walked away disappointed, but not completely. She had checked off another block on her never-ending list of to-do-s in this case.

When she finished her houses, she met Wyatt and Shea at Wyatt's truck. "So, you guys come up with anything?"

Wyatt nodded. "Yes, the Flynn's down the street were having a roof put on the day Blare disappeared. There were two workmen, and I've got their contact information."

"Good." Shea wiped sweat off his brow. "We need to interview them. Can you get Jaiden to locate them and give Reggie and me the location they're working at tomorrow? We can stop by and interview them on the job."

"Sure." Wyatt texted the request to Jaiden.

Shea scratched his jaw; his expression one Reggie knew as dismayed. "There's a regular ice cream truck that operates along this street. The guy does a couple rounds each day, one in the afternoon and one in the morning. A neighbor told me she thought it was weird the truck cruised through in the morning, earlier than normal."

Wyatt tossed his hat into the truck. "Text Leo the company name. Leo will research them and send you the driver's contact information."

"Great. Thanks, Wyatt. Shea and I will talk with him tomorrow." Reggie looked at her phone notes. "The Farmers across the street and down had a cable installer at their house that day. His name is Bo Bennett, and they gave me his card. We'll go talk with him tomorrow too."

"Anyone get anything else?" Wyatt asked, looking haggard and as worried as Reggie had ever seen her old friend. This extended case was getting to her old pal. No wonder, he not only cared deeply for his township. He and Sage had a five-year-old son, Ty, of their own. She could only imagine how parents must feel right now.

"Much as Reggie and I want kids, this shit scares the devil out of me. I can't imagine how you and Sage must feel." Shea slapped a loving arm around Wyatt's shoulder.

Wyatt nodded sadly then turned to his phone to read. "Yeah, thanks. Leo texted that he spoke with the postal worker. He's a substitute, filling in for the regular. Her name is Joe Fin, and he's texting you her home address and phone number now. She's been off . . . on disability . . . since the date the kid vanished."

Reggie's brows went up. "Strange . . . coincidence."

Shea's head jerked. "No such thing. We're going to visit her tomorrow."

Reggie rocked her head forward. "Definitely."

CHAPTER 8

Reggie, Shea and Wyatt drank coffee at Wyatt's desk, planning their day. The phone on his desk rang. Wyatt glanced at the coroner's number on the screen and picked up the receiver. "Sheriff Gordon, morning, Doc. How goes it?"

He listened for a minute then interjected, "Hang on, Doc. Reggie and Shea are here. No need for you to repeat this, when we can all hear it at the same time." Wyatt clicked a button and laid the handset down.

The aging coroner's gruff voice sounded through the speaker. "Morning, law dogs. Hope you're all faring well"

After a round of, "Good morning, Doc," the physician took over. "I've got news for you, but first I want to ask you a couple questions. You know, this Coronavirus thing has been copying the Black Death. That's downright plagiarism."

"Geez, Doc, do you start every conversation with bad jokes?" Reggie groaned.

A chuckle answered over the speaker. Shea was prepared for him. "Hey, Doc, you know jokes about death aren't funny . . . unless they're executed properly."

Doc cackled over the line. "I see you've been boning up on your death humor, Marshal Montgomery. Well done. Do you realize humas fear hippos because they're violent and responsible for hundreds of deaths each year?"

Reggie grinned at her husband. "Seriously?"

"Seriously," he came back. "In reality, people kill people way more per year. That notion is simply hippo-critical." He guffawed.

"Okay," Wyatt rolled his eyes. "You've got humor off your chest, bad as it is. Can we get down to business?"

"Sure thing, Sheriff. The DNA for all three victims came back, along with DNA found on fibers in their mouths. The freshest victim's fibers had not only her DNA on it, but that of the other two victims, as well. I suspected this, from my preliminary examination under the microscope. There was a third DNA present that doesn't belong to any of the three. It has not been identified. Fibers in the middle-aged corpse's mouth contained her DNA, that of the oldest corpse and DNA from the same unidentified person. The oldest corpse's mouth held fibers that contained her DNA and DNA from the unidentified person."

"What are you saying, Doc?" Reggie frowned. "Does this mean there's a fourth victim we have not found yet?"

"Possibly. It is not something I can confirm. Fibers were identified as from a pillow. Death was from asphyxiation for all three victims. I can confirm a pillow appears to have been the murder weapon."

Shea winced. "The girls were smothered to death with a pillow."

"It appears so, and with a single pillow. All three of them must've used that pillow, it was then used to kill them. There were no signs of struggle. They must've been asleep at the time of death."

"Can we get the DNA strings immediately?" Reggie sat straight.

Magnolia Blossoms

"Of course, I've just sent the files to you three and to Carla Orson at NCMEC."

"Great," Shea chewed the corner of his mouth. "Carla can run the DNA through the missing child database to see if she gets any hits. I'll have it run through the U. S. Marshall's database."

"I'll have my team run it through the FBI database as well. If there's DNA on file for the missing girls, we should find out who they are before long. Then we can determine what they have in common, besides their method of demise." At least they were moving forward on the serial killer case.

"Thanks, Doc. Talk with you later." Wyatt's attempt to get off the phone before Doc went stand-up comic on them again didn't work.

"Sure thing, Wyatt, anything I can do. Say the word. Hey, do you know what the calendar said on its death bed?"

"I'm afraid you're going to tell me." Wyatt moaned.

"My days are numbered."

"Aren't those of all of us?" Reggie laughed, as Wyatt hung up the phone. She turned to Shea. "Tell Carla and the Marshal's office to search not only the ages the girls were when they were killed, but to go back for six-to-eight years. The number six keeps coming up. There's six years between the ages of the victims—six, twelve and eighteen-years old. This number is significant."

Lynda Rees

CHAPTER 9

Later that afternoon Shea parked his truck in front of Bo Bennet's house, the cable installer who had been working at a house a block from the Moore house when Blare Moore disappeared. First thing that registered with Reggie, a small, ragged looking magnolia tree was attempting to take root in the front yard. It had clearly been having a problem doing so, though it was properly staked and mulched.

They exited the truck. Bennet answered the door, as they had hoped he would. His headquarters had told them it was Bo's day off.

"Mr. Bennet, I'm FBI Special Agent Reggie Montgomery, and this is my associate U. S. Marshal Shea Montgomery. We are investigating the disappearance of Blare Moore. We'd like to ask you a few questions."

The plump but solid looking six-footer smiled and motioned them inside with a sad expression on his face. "I sure hope you find that poor kid."

"Yes, we're working hard to do just that. Maybe you can be of assistance." Shea stood beside his wife in Bennet's sparse living room. It looked as though random items had been plucked from their spaces and disappeared. Walls sported bright evidence of frames being recently removed, where paint had faded from exposure to sunlight and other elements around them.

"Would you like something to drink?" Bennet offered, waving an arm as invitation to sit on what was left of his living room furniture.

"No, thank you. We'll only take a moment of your time." Reggie wasn't here for a social call, though it was customary in the south to offer food and at least a drink to visitors, welcomed or not. "I noticed your tree outside. Pitiful thing doesn't appear to be doing well."

Bo's face went sadder than before. "Yeah, I bought that damned magnolia tree for my wife on our fifth anniversary, just before she hightailed it out of town with some dude she met on the internet. Bitch took half my stuff and all our savings. I hope that damned tree rots where it stands."

The vehement in his voice and sentiment were clearly not meant for the tree, but for his wife. "I'm sorry to hear that, Mr. Bennet."

Bo shrugged. "I'm better off without her. Learned my lesson."

Shea changed the subject. "We understand you were working in the Moore's neighborhood the day Blare disappeared."

Bo nodded, stuffing hands into his short's pockets. "Yeah, I was on the next block. The mother was sitting on the front steps and the kid was playing in the yard when I drove by on the way to my first job. I remember thinking if my wife hadn't lost our first baby, our little girl might be her age by now. They looked happy."

Reggie controlled the hope starting to surge through her veins. "How did that make you feel?"

Bo's brows rose, and he smiled. "Actually, grateful. It's probably best things worked out the way they did. I would hate to be stuck with that bitch, raising a family with her when she clearly didn't love me enough. I was a damned fool."

Reggie's wave of hope dissipated. "I'm sorry for your situation, Mr. Bennet. It's difficult going through a breakup. At least you have an opportunity for a fresh start."

"Yeah, but it's going to be a long while before I trust another female. Sorry, ma'am, no offense."

"None taken." Reggie waved a hand. "Did you notice anything or anyone suspicious as you drove or while you were on the job?

"No, I didn't see another soul, and when I was working, I was mostly in and out of the house on the other side, so the street in front of their house wasn't visible. By the time I finished that job, that block was cordoned off, and there were police everywhere. That gorgeous Native American Deputy stopped me and asked what I'd seen, but I wasn't much help."

Shea nodded. "Jaiden Coldwater. Yes, we read her report. We're requestioning everyone in case someone remembered something more."

Reggie and Shea extended business cards to Bo. She shook his hand after he accepted them. "Thanks for talking with us. Please reach out to one of us day or night, should you recall anything else."

"Will do." Bo opened the door for them to exit.

Outside in Shea's truck, Reggie checked off another block on her to-do list. "Well, that wasn't much help."

"Yeah, I thought maybe we had something on the serial killer investigation when I spotted that tree. I don't take Bo Bennet for being involved in either case."

"Yeah, me either." She eyed her handsome husband, touching her diamond necklace. "Who do you want to tackle next?"

"Leo and Jaiden interrogated the roofers, Matt Ryan and Bubba Evans, working on a house a couple blocks down when Blare vanished. They saw nothing strange, but they did say the ice cream truck that works the area went by in the morning. Bubba, the owner of the roofing company, said he knew the guy patrolled in the afternoons and sometimes evenings. He thought it odd that he'd gone by so early." Shea read the deputy's report on his phone.

"Did Leo or Jaiden get the driver's information?" It sounded fishy to Reggie too.

"Sure did. Leo said the driver owns the truck. He got his address and name. Harvey Cool lives a couple blocks from here."

"Great." She smiled. "Mr. Cool is our next stop.

Shea drove in silence until they arrived at Cool's house. The tiny row house had a postage-sized yard with an ancient iron fence. The miniature lot barely had room for a slim walkway along one side, and the opposite outside wall of the house appeared to signify the property's border. A satellite dish awkwardly positioned on the roof near the front of the house. The block of similarly designed homes. This one differentiated itself with the front entrance nearly enclosed by massive magnolia trees growing too close to the structure. As though trying to make up for their intrusion, mature trees proudly sprouted fragrant blossoms.

Reggie's heart skipped a beat, and she instinctively toned it down. "Shows promise," she uttered as Shea opened her door and took her hand to help her out. He was a gentleman always, and she adored him for it.

"Yeah, I saw them too." He followed her to the front stoop where she pushed the doorbell.

A shaggy, pudgy, mid-fifties man in plaid shorts and a white wife-beater style, underwear shirt answered the door. Curly grey hair curled around his shirt's edges, as though trying to escape from their confines. A scrubby double chin on his lack-luster, wrinkled face added to his unkempt appearance. He clearly wasn't ready for visitors.

"Yeah?" his gruff voice grumbled, leaning on the half-opened door.

She made introductions, and they flashed their badges. "May we come in a few minutes?"

Harvey hesitated, glanced over his shoulder then back at them, standing back and opening the door wider. "What the hell? Come on in."

The room's furnishings consisted of an aged easy chair beside a small table with an attached lamp and dusty looking shade. A crate across the room from the chair held a flat-screen television tuned to the racing channel. Several stacks of racing forms piled in stacks around the room, and one lay open on the side table beside a half-empty beer bottle and a bag of chips. No pictures, paintings or knickknacks. A phone laid on the table.

Clearly this dude was a bachelor, and his appearance showed his lack of changing the status. Reggie explained why they were there.

"I don't know nothing about that."

"That may be true, but anything at all you might've seen could be important. I understand you patrolled the neighborhood earlier than anormal that day. What time did you go by the Moore house?"

He rubbed his scruffy jaw. "I recon it was about ten thirty."

"Is that your normal time?" Shea questioned.

"Nah, I usually cruise through that neighborhood about three-thirty, after the little turds get home from school. If it is a good day, I swing through again around eight, when they're dying for dessert."

Reggie nodded. "Did you see anyone or anything unusual, and why so early that day?"

Harvey glanced at his easy chair. "I had money on a horse, I went to the track that afternoon to watch the race in person."

Shea's brow furrowed. "The Louisville track? What horse?"

"Nah, Kentucky Downs. Dakota Power, he's a Mane Lane Farm racehorse, a local breeder."

She smiled. "Yes, the owner, Levi Madison, is a friend. I know the horse. He's something else." She made note to check race results.

He chuckled, losing some of the obvious tension he'd been holding. "Yeah, I won big. It was worth missing the afternoon route." He frowned. "Listen, I don't know nothing to help you folks. I saw that rug rat and her ma in front of the house. The kid perked up. It looked like she was asking for a treat. Her ma shot it down quickly. I know the signs. It weren't a good time for ice cream; but hell, it's the only time I had available. I did not want to miss the race. Few people around. I slipped through without making a damned dime."

Shea squirreled his mouth to the side. "You don't like kids?"

"Hell, I freaking love 'em. At least, I love the money. They're easy targets for sweets, but no. The little urchins are a pain in the ass. I'm glad they have a sweet tooth."

Shea nodded. "Would you mind if I used your restroom?"

Reggie knew he did not need to pee. Shea wanted to stroll through this dude's house and look for evidence."

Cool rolled eyes and pushed out a huff. "Guess not. It's off the dining room." He waved a hand past the living room to a space showing no signs he had used it as anything but storage for old racing forms, piled high in stacks around the walls. Shea disappeared on his quest.

Reggie considered their other case. "Your trees are certainly in full bloom out front. They nearly cover your door."

Cool glanced toward the front of his home. "Yeah, son-of-a-bitches are out of hand. I keep trying to train them off the entrance, but they are old and strong. Completely blocked the front window and they are taking over, brushing the gutters and roof. I keep complaining to my property owner, but that prick does not give a shit. He'll care when he has to replace the roof."

Obviously, the trees had no sentimental significance for Harvey Cool. Shea returned, they thanked Mr. Cool for his time. He grumbled a response and exited to Harvey's slamming and lock clicking. Shea took a quick run behind the house and returned.

Once in the truck, Shea turned to Reggie. "No sign of anything in the kitchen, dining room or bath. No inside basement door, and no outside entrance to a basement out back."

"Must be a slab house." She bit her lip. "What do you think about Harvey Cool?"

Shea appeared to consider a moment then met her gaze "He's a confirmed bachelor. Hates kids. A slob. I believe he's too lazy to come up with a kidnapping scheme, even if he were in debt for his gambling problem. Leo checked. Cool has no known financial problems."

She nodded agreement. "He could be indebted to a bookie. That wouldn't be in his financial records. If he needed cash, he would've asked for ransom by now." She heaved a sigh. "Cool's not the emotional type. He would not care enough to grab a kid to molest. If he did, he wouldn't bother to care for her like the serial killer did his victims. Like you said, Harvey Cool's lazy."

"Yes, I agree. He's not good for the serial kills, but he had opportunity and potential motive for the child abduction. We can't rule him out on Blare Moore's case."

She agreed. "Yeah, you're right; but I just don't see it."

"Me either, but stranger things have happened." He started the engine.

"Let us visit Willie Holden next." Her head bobbed, and he pulled out onto the road. Moments later they were on the other end of town in a seedy tenement-type complex. Willie Holden's apartment was in the basement level of a twelve-unit building. The hallway reeked of dirt and urine.

Reggie cringed as she knocked on the disgustingly dirty door, hoping their bottle of disinfectant in Shea's truck was full.

The door cracked, and two chains kept it from swinging wide, as a wrinkled, darkly tanned face met their gaze. "What the hell do you coppers want?"

A known felon, this pervert was on the known pedophile list. The deviate had spent three years behind bars for molesting three young boys. He would know from their looks; they were law enforcement.

"Open the door, Willie. We need to talk." She introduced herself and Shea, as they flashed their badges at him, and he undid the line of chain locks. Stepping back, he made way for them to enter. His two-room residence was visible from the entrance, sparsely furnished with a white-sheeted mattress on the floor of one room, a lap beside it. A pile of clothing lay in a corner. The entry room had two wooden chairs and a small table, cluttered with newspapers, a dirty dish and coffee cup. The open-topped plastic trash can was full, containing an assortment of beer bottles and other items. Ragged blankets covered windows. No pictures, personal items, couch or television."

"What the fuck do you want?" Willie was clearly not happy to see them, but he knew the routine. On parole and on the state's pedophile list, he had to know he was subject to visit and search at any time.

She studied his eyes without emotion. "You're aware of the Blare Moore case."

"The missing kid? Yeah. Who isn't? It's all over the news."

Shea stood to Willie's other side. "No television or radio. How do you get the news?" They had checked, and Willie had no personal vehicle.

"Radio' always on at the car wash where I work. They blast that shit every half hour. This little shit hole of a town does not get much news. When they do, they inundate you with it."

Big word for a guy who washes cars. Then again, Willie Holden had been an accountant before he had been caught making porn films with neighborhood boys.

"You don't like it here. Why do you stay?"

"You know the answer to that, bitch cop." He glared at her. "Can't leave town until my parole is up."

Shea's fists balled at his side, and his shoulders puffed up. "Watch your language, Holden."

Willie cocked one brow as he looked Shea up and down. Shea towered over the five-ten-or-so degenerate. Where Shea was tall and lanky but muscled, Holden was thin and ill-fed. He did not appear to have lifted anything weightier than a drying rag at the car wash. His stature backed down appropriately, then he moved focus to Reggie.

"Sorry, ma'am. I ain't been in that vicinity, anywhere near that kid."

Shea's voice was icy. "We know you like boys. What about girls?"

"Look, man, I'm going to court-ordered counseling. I never miss a meeting with my parole officer. I am working six days a week. I got no social life. I've not been near a school, day care or touched a kid since I got out of the joint. I'm not going back."

Yeah, right. His sort rarely changed. He had a taste for it. Eventually, if not now, he would succumb to his urges. Reggie wasn't convinced. "Where were you the day Blare Moore disappeared?"

"I was at the car wash. It was a pretty day. We were slammed. Ask my manager." Holden turned to the table then shoved a business card for the facility toward Reggie. She glanced at it and slipped it into the pocket of her navy blazer.

"Be sure, we will." Ice had not melted in Shea's voice.

"If you remember anything, if you hear or see anything that might help us locate Blare Moore, contact one of us." Reggie and Shea handed Willie their cards.

He tossed them onto the pile of mail and papers on the table. "Will do." He walked toward the door, as though ushering them out. They were heading that direction anyway.

"Until later." Shea's goodbye held a warning. He too, understood the rarity of a true pedophile cured of his hunger for molesting children. Once a pervert, always a pervert. Involved in this case, the serial killer case or not, Willie Holden would someday find his way back to a cell. She was sure of it.

In the truck, she revealed her opinion. "I'm not sure about him. We need to check his alibi and talk with his boss and probation officer. I am uneasy about him. Guilt oozes from his pores, but I'm not sure he's our man . . . for either case."

Shea frowned. "Still, we can't rule him out."

"No, we certainly can't." She released a heavy breath and made a note on her phone.

Lynda Rees

CHAPTER 10

The following day Shea helped Reggie into his truck. "Well, Willie Holden's alibi holds up, and his parole officer has confidence in him not being near any kids. He seemed competent."

She waited for Shea to climb into the driver's seat. "Yeah, but that dude still gives me the creeps."

"Me too." Shea squeezed her hand. "Wyatt spoke with Buddy Elbert, the U. S. Postal Worker who is covering the route where the Moore family lives. He's new and a floater. He's just filling in and wasn't working the day Blare went missing. The regular delivery person is Joey Fin, who went on disability the day after Blare's disappearance. Let's go talk with Joey."

"Sounds good." She pulled up Wyatt's message on her phone, which included the address for Joe Fin, and gave directions to Shea. Moments later, they parked in front of a spacious yard with a white picket fence around it. A wide side lawn surrounded a mature magnolia tree. Two smaller ones flanked corners of the back of the lot. The two-story, plank house had a broad, red-trimmed porch with tufted cushions on a swing, a small table and a tufted cushioned rocker. Red shutters framed windows, and the door matched, setting off white paint. It was a pleasant looking home.

"Homey." Shea helped her out of the truck cab.

"Yeah, I could live in a home like this." Her husband trailed her to the door.

A thirty-something man answered, wearing jeans and a dark tee shirt. His well-kempt appearance was drastic against appearance of their past interviewees. "Are you Joe Fin?" Reggie flipped her badge. Shea did the same.

The man smiled and swung the screen door open. "No, I'm Dillon, Joey's husband. Please, come in."

They stepped inside, and the screen door clicked closed behind them. Dillon didn't bother shutting the door.

A petite, short, curly-haired brunette sat on a couch, her casted leg propped atop pillows on a coffee table. Floral scene paintings decorated the room. Fluffy cushions and side chairs matched the sofa. Lamps occupied end tables. The home had a woman's touch.

"Joey, these officers would like to see you." He indicated they should sit, and they each took a chair. Dillon sat beside his wife. Reggie made introductions and explained why they were there.

"I'm not sure I can tell you anything that would help. I remember seeing Mrs. Moore and Blare that day, though at the time, I didn't know the child's name. Mrs. Moore was sitting on the stoop, so I handed her their mail. We didn't have many words, only a 'hello' and 'thank you.' The girl looked up from her dolls when I walked by, but she did not say anything and neither did I. I figured they had told her not to talk with strangers. I never speak to people's kids unless they imply it's okay."

"Was anyone else around that day? Did you notice anything out of the ordinary?" Shea focused on the woman.

Magnolia Blossoms

Joey and her husband acted at ease. "No, nothing. Like I told the officer that day, everything seemed normal. There was extraordinarily little traffic, and few people were around outside. I wish I could help you find that poor, little darling. I can only imagine how her parents must feel and what she's going through." Her face winced up. Dillion slipped a hand over hers.

Reggie switched subjects. "You have a lovely home. I noticed you have several magnolia trees. They're lovely this time of year."

Joe smiled and turned it on her husband then back to them. "Yes, we bought this place when we married a couple years ago. I loved the big tree in the yard so much, Dillion has bought me one each year after that for our anniversary. The two are planted in corners of the back yard."

Reggie smiled. "That's sweet, romantic. So, you have been married a couple years now. Any children?"

The couple's eyes met, and they smiled some private communication between themselves. Joe turned to them. "Not yet. We're just starting to work on that."

"Good for you." Reggie felt happy for the couple and jealous at the same time. They had what she and Shea had been striving for. "What happened to your leg?"

Joey's nose curled. "We were four wheeling at a friend's farm. I made a too-quick turn and flipped my bike. It's broken just above the ankle."

"It could've been worse." Dillion winced. "She's lucky."

"Yes, I'll have to be more careful next time." Her gaze locked on Dillion's, and they both smiled.

"Would you mind showing us your ATVs?" Shea stood. "We're thinking of getting a couple."

Dillion followed suit. "No problem."

So did Reggie. They followed Dillion through the dining room. A glass-topped table was surrounded by modern, cushioned chairs. A glass-topped buffet held stylish China and glassware. The kitchen was granite, stainless appliances and black cabinetry. Through French doors, they exited to a large deck and down three steps to the lawn. Dillion unlocked a small, double car garage. Inside sat two all-terrain vehicles, sparkling clean.

"Here are our babies." Dillion's voice rang of pride.

"Nice." Shea inspected the vehicles, walking around each of them, touching occasionally as though admiring and whistling. "Very nice."

She knelt and studied the tires. "So, you and Joey ride often? Where do you go?"

"Farmland owned by a couple friends. Sometimes to parks like Land Between The Lakes."

"Would you mind if we made an impression of these tires? They look sturdy. I'd like to make sure we get something like this on our quads, when we do buy them." Shea grinned, acting enthusiastic.

"Not at all, but I think this tire is standard on this make and model."

Shea didn't wait for Dillion to question his motive. He trotted to his truck and got a mold kit. Reggie continued to investigate the bikes, while Shea quickly molded the tread. "Thanks."

"Sure." Dillion looked confused but didn't ask.

Reggie took over. "Well, thanks for your help. Please, thank Joey for me. I hope she heals quickly." She extended a card to him.

"Will do." He accepted cards from Reggie and Shea. "Nice meeting you folks. Hope you find that child."

Once inside their truck, Shea fired the engine to life. Reggie eyed him. "We need to investigate every shop that sells or works on ATVs. I don't know if these two participate in the serial killing, but whomever buried those girls took them to that property on a quad."

CHAPTER 11

Wyatt, Shea and Reggie sipped coffee in Wyatt's office. "Thanks for meeting me here. It's a mess. The mayor is on my ass and so is the Governor. They want this serial killer caught."

"I understand. The Director is on my case about it too, but more pressing is the missing child. We've got to find that kid, even if chances are she's dead by now." Reggie's voice must've sounded as desperate as she felt.

Shea grabbed her free hand and held it securely on his thigh. "It's been too long. Carla with NCMAC hasn't found any clues yet either."

Wyatt leaned back in his desk chair. "Let's go over the facts, one case at a time. The magnolia tree is significant. One marked each grave. That means something. We don't know what." He made notes on a whiteboard behind his desk.

Reggie sat her cup down. "They each appear to have bene planted at the time of burial based on age and maturity of the trees. This was someone local who knows the land is vacant. According to Wyatt, no one has touched it for about thirty-five-years, and the heirs aren't local. It would be unlikely for anyone to hunt there with No Trespassing signs up. They were sure to pick a spot unlikely for discovery. No traditional grave markers, only trees."

Shea released her hand. "This killer is smart. Most are. We have checked with every seller in the area. None produced anything that might lead us to the purchaser."

Wyatt wrote that on the board. "No missing children of the approximate age of the first victim have bene found in Sweetwater or surrounding counties. Carla's national database and that of the FBI have found no twelve-to-thirteen-year-old of her description recently disappeared. The same for the other two victims."

Reggie frowned. "I've told Carla and my team to expand that search to go back further. The victims were approximately six years apart. That is significant. We should expand database search parameters for maybe eight years earlier than their ages of death. It seems to me, one might've replaced another, and so on. Each of these girls could've been a replacement for one who had grown too old."

"Too old for what?" Shea's brow furrowed toward her.

"I don't know. Whatever the killer wanted. They were all dressed oddly in child-like clothing, homemade frilly dresses with white anklets. Lace hand-sewn around the cuff of their socks. No shoes. Hair in pigtails with ribbons tied around them. Those poor girls appeared to be sleeping peacefully, wrapped in their large square of a floral-print, cotton, fabric."

Wyatt nodded. "She's onto something. Each victim appeared well-tended, not violently killed. No signs of sexual abuse."

Shea bit his lip. "Twelve-to-thirteen, she was at the precipice, ready to begin puberty."

Magnolia Blossoms

Reggie placed both hands on top of the desk. "The killer didn't want the girl to grow up. He wanted her to stay young. But why?"

Wyatt wrote on the board. "Yes, why? That's the important question."

Shea continued to chew his lip, looking down as though studying something "Each girl has similar scar tissue buildup around an ankle, as though she'd worn a thick, heavy cuff of some kind around it over a prolonged period of time."

Reggie's heart ached, and she struggled to keep emotion tapped down. "They were confined. Probably locked away somewhere and chained to something sturdy so they couldn't try to dig or fight their way out."

Wyatt continued writing, his strong, broad back to them. "There was no sign of struggle. They were sleeping or drugged, though TOD and decomp did not allow for finding out with what . . . if anything. Smothered . . . with their own pillow, . . . and died of asphyxiation.

"Doc's report based on examination of oral cavities, shows it was likely a feather pillow. It appears the same pillow was slept on by all three victims, and it was the murder weapon for their executions. The killer did not want them to fight. He didn't want to see their faces as they died . . . he cared too much for them." Her profiling skills were working on high speed. She was getting into the killer's head. "He dressed and wrapped them with care, covering their faces, so he didn't have to see them in death any longer than necessary. He gave them an honorable burial in beautiful surrounds and marked their graves with trees so he could locate them. Come visit them. Pay respects. Magnolia trees."

Wyatt finished writing and turned. "Oddly, spores recovered from their nostrils prove there is DNA from a fourth person. Someone else besides these girls used that pillow."

"The killer?" Shea threw out a bone.

"Maybe, or another victim." It burned her soul to say those words.

"And we haven't found her. Either her grave is so old and hidden without a marker or she's buried somewhere else." Wyatt plopped into his seat.

"The number six keeps playing in this. There's six years approximately between these girls." Her phone chirped. She checked the screen. "I need to take this." She clicked it on, and the men sat silently while she finished the call. Finally, she clicked off. "It was my team. They've identified the three girls and reached out to their families. Each of the victims vanished when they were approximately six years old. They were missing around six years before they were slain in this piece of shit ritual of by our wacko butcher." With each word, her pitch grew higher.

"Son-of-a-bitch, this puzzle is starting to fall into place." Wyatt slammed a fist on the desktop.

"The killer took them at six and wanted them to stay that age. Why?" Reggie's gut was doing acrobatics she could not force down.

They were onto a significant clue. She was sure of it.

CHAPTER 12

Reggie and Shea soon learned from her FBI team the newest victim of the three had disappeared six years prior from Bonnyville, the next town to the south of Sweetwater. She'd been almost seven years old. Sure enough, the second victim died around the time the newest one was abducted. The second had disappeared six years prior around the time the oldest cadaver had been murdered. That poor child had disappeared from Benton, a small lakeside town near to Sweetwater.

Shea gritted his teeth before speaking. "Each girl was between six and seven years old when they disappeared. That was a span of eighteen years . . . at least . . . that this son-of-a-bitch has been operating in this area. How did this go on without being noticed?"

Reggie was reading the same report. "Yes, the first abduction happened eighteen years ago from Sweetwater. Her replacement was abducted twelve years ago, and the older girl was killed. Six years later, the newest was taken; and the second victim was slain. Without their bodies, it was difficult to put the puzzle together. You know as well as I do. Children of all ages disappear all the time. Making a connection between them is why we were stationed here in the first place.”

“I'm not sure about you, but I'm all for taking these roles back permanently. Agree?”

Why six years?

“Oh, yeah, sure. We want these roles back. Guess we'd best get serious about purchasing a home in the vicinity. In the meantime, we've got a killer to catch and a missing child to locate.”

Shea sighed and laid down his phone. “As always in our cases, the job takes precedence. The missing kid is our prime concern, though after this time it's likely she won't be found alive. Chances are the serial killer won't kill again for another six years.”

“The serial killer's MO is he kidnaps a girl child around six years old, holds the kid captive for six years, then smothers the child and replaces her with a newly kidnapped six-year-old girl.” She put her cell on the table and turned to a whiteboard and wrote the number six in large letters at the top.”

Could Blare be the substitute for the last victim?

Shea met her gaze as she turned. “Are you thinking what I'm thinking? Every six years, he replaces his captive with a new girl approximately six-years old.”

She smiled. “Blare Moore is that age. She could still be alive if the serial killer has her.”

Sparkle in Shea's eyes proved they were on the same wavelength. “Exactly.”

She spun to face the murder board, renewed hope in her heart. She'd been thinking it off and on, but it had finally come into focus. Possibility of Blare having survived over the course of the last three weeks renewed Reggie's fighting spirit. “We must work quickly.” She wrote as she spoke. “Why six? Why keep her for six? Why kill her at all? Why a girl and not a boy?”

Magnolia Blossoms

Shea rubbed his square jaw. "Something happened in the killer's life six years prior to his first kill. We need to learn what."

Reggie completed his thought. "Whatever it was had to do with a girl child."

"A daughter, perhaps . . . a six-year-old girl child." Shea was becoming hopeful too. His sparkling eyes told her as they met hers.

"Yes," she beamed. That would explain why a girl instead of a boy and why that age. The killer is replacing his lost girl child."

"Why kill her at twelve-to-thirteen? Why kill her at all?" She's brows furrowed.

"Perhaps he killed his own six-year-old daughter . . . on purpose . . . or by accident. He could be reliving that kill each time."

Shea's head shook. "We can't rule that out, but he's not killing the victims at that age. He's killing them at twelve-to-thirteen."

She nodded somberly, her lower lip out as she considered that. "He wants them to stay little. Why would six be important, if he lets them live approximately six years in captivity?" Ideas were swarming through her head. They'd been flittering around in her brain for the last couple weeks like lost puzzle pieces finally starting to find their homes on the board. Slowly.

Too slowly.

She let out a heavy sigh. "At the killing age, they're starting to enter puberty. They were possibly beginning menses. They have been well-cared for, so they are developing naturally. That means growing breasts, maybe becoming more defiant."

Shea nodded. "They'd be stronger, harder to control . . . if after all that time, they still had the desire to escape. Some captives lose that, as they become acclimated to captivity. He could've convinced them they were alone in the world, and he was the only one left to care for them."

She met his eyes. "You're talking about Stockholm Syndrome. Trauma bonding, obtaining a victim's loyalty. That makes sense, especially if he is convinced the child her parents do not want her any more or have died somehow. Also, there's Maslow's Hierarchy that might come into play over time. He plays on her psychological needs . . . in order." She wrote these terms on the board and continued talking and writing. "First of all, he'd need to see to her physiological needs—shelter, clothing, food, water and sleep. He'd tell her he was putting her somewhere safe . . . maybe so whomever killed her parents can't get to her. Then he would work on her safety needs—personal security, health, property . . . maybe supplying her with entertainment, toys, books, music . . . things that make her feel secure."

Shea took over. "She'd then need belonging and love. He'd convince her he was her friend, her new family and try to become intimate with her to provide a sense of connection."

She nodded as she wrote. "Yes, like they're in this together. They belong together. In this case, intimacy doesn't involve sexual encounters." She released a huff of hot air.

Shea gave her time to write as he wrote. "He'd play on her self-esteem, show her respect, recognition for being a good girl . . . not resisting or trying to get away . . . rewarding good behavior with special treats. He would make it worth it for her to be the best child he could have. This all makes her pliable, manageable and less trouble to keep captive."

The marker clicked as she speed-wrote on the board. "The killer is smart. He understands psychology and uses it to his advantage—to keep his captives malleable, compliant. A six-year-old child is impressionable, easy for an expert to influence and manipulate." She spun and beamed at her husband, feeling confident they were beginning to understand the killer's motivation.

Please, let us be right about Blare. Let her live.

It was a relief she could let out emotion when she and Shea were alone. It did not fog her thinking, but he understood better than anyone how tough it was to shove your feelings to the back burner for work. It was a necessity in their jobs, however. They were equally good at it.

"I want to interview Blare Moore's mother again. We're missing something important, and it's starting with her."

She shoved her phone in her blazer pocket and ran for the door, Shea hot on her heels. All the while, she tamped down her feelings. Must not excite the mother. Do not give her false hope.

CHAPTER 13

Reggie followed her husband into the tenth retailer of ATVs for the day. Besides sellers, they had also interviewed every mechanic in or around Sweetwater who worked on ATVs. So far, they had learned a lot about them, but as before they were about to have to listen to yet another salesman expound on, what the average person doesn't know about ATV's. She braced herself when jingle of the entrance door rang and a smiling, slick-haired, logo-shirted man strolled toward them with hand out and perfect teeth bared in a practiced smile.

"How can I help you folks?" He handed Shea a card.

Reggie stood back, letting Shea take the lead, though it sickened her that salespeople always thought the man was the one who did vehicle shopping for them both.

"We're looking for a particular tread on an off the road vehicle. Can you tell me about the type of tire we might be looking for?"

"Well, sir, I'm glad you came in today. We have a sale on all-terrain tires."

"Why would I want all-terrain vs. something specific?" Shea asked.

"Well, Mr.—" The inevitable pause, waiting for a name.

"Montgomery, Shea Montgomery."

"Mr. Montgomery, you'll want to figure out the type of terrain you are planning on riding on. That enables you to purchase the best tire for your use. Now if you find yourself in thick mud one weekend and rough, hilly trails the next, all-terrain is the way to go."

"What about sand?" Shea cued him.

"If you're hitting the dunes with your four-wheeler, no ordinary tire is going to cut it. To keep up with your pals and keep your wheels turning, you need specially designed ATV sand tires or paddle tires. Sand tires have paddles for grip. Front sand tires have a center rib or smooth tread. Rear paddles provide grip and stability to cut through loose surfaces like sand, snow or silt. The front tires give you light, precise steering to navigate it without getting stuck. Maximum flotation keeps your wheels from spinning. Your tire stays atop the sand instead of sinking in. Sand is forced under the tire s the ATV floats on it. This is the difference between flying over dunes and being stuck in a rut. Your tires run cooler through the desert, maintaining a longer lifespan of the tire."

Shea nodded and began to look at a display, the salesperson at his heels. "So, if I'm in mud a lot, I might need a mud tire?"

The guy grinned. "Absolutely. Specialized ATV mud tires are the best for riding through mud. They have many features you won't find on other types of tires. The biggest benefit of mud tires is wide tread pattern allowing them to grip the road and prevent slipping and sliding. When you encounter mud and other unpredictable terrains, you don't want to have to worry about getting stuck."

Shea shook his head. "That wouldn't work. No. So tell me more about . . . What did you call it? All-terrain tires?"

It was all Reggie could do to keep from laughing.

"Well now. Those are our best-selling ATV tires. Yes Siree. You can't beat a good all-terrain tire. Where the type of tire you buy should depend on the terrain you intend to ride, you can't go wrong with a good all-terrain tire. For premium performance, it's essential to equip your machine with the best tires suited to your adventures, but when your paths tend to differ, an all-terrain ATV tire is the way to go. If you're weeping through sand dunes one week and the next, you're riding rocky plains, you're equipped to handle it all. One reason is the type of premium rubber used to manufacture these tires. The other is a particular type of traction. Oftentimes, all-terrain ATV tires have a longer lifespan than their counterparts. They tend to perform better at higher speeds and are smooth riding. When selecting an all-terrain tire, to maximize speed, I'd suggest you select a lighter weight tire."

"I see." Shea scratched his chin, looking undecided.

"So, are you ready to take a look at some rubber?" The salesperson slapped Shea's back and ushered him away from the ones he'd been staring at. They were meant for something much smaller than what Shea and Reggie were looking for.

She stopped leaning on the countertop and followed the two men to the back of the showroom. As they passed flashy, shiny machines by the dozens, she glanced specifically at their treads.

The salesperson stopped them in front of a display along a wall split into three parts. "So, where will you be riding this machine, and do you already have one?"

"Yeah, just interested in the tires. All-terrain, or mud. Not sure yet."

The man pointed at a display of rubber. "These are our best all-terrain tires. That might be the way you should go."

Shea pulled the folded photograph out of his back pocket. "Actually, I'd like something with a tread like this." He handed the unfolded picture to the salesperson.

"Yeah, that's our Dirt Digger tire. It's the best-selling ATV tire we carry. Our customers love extra traction it gives from the directional tread design. This baby will perform in petty much any grit or grim you put her through." He eyed Shea with a satisfied look, already calculating his commission on four tires.

Now comes the upsell. She bit her lip.

"Now, if you want a more lightweight tire, the Corbin ATV489 features open tread with outstanding cleanout, to keep you moving even in the stickiest mud. Rounded contour gives you superior cornering and maneuverability. It's made in the USA and an exceptional tire. Then there's the Quarter 350 Ultra with an open and non-directional tread that will give you superior traction, even wear and long life regardless the terrain. It's excellent with a unique design to provide amazing shock absorption and stability. That makes for a smoother more enjoyable ride. Looking for peace of mind, you can't beat her."

Shea moved toward the Dirt Digger display. "I think this is the one that made the track in the photograph. What do you say, sweetheart?" He turned to Reggie, patiently leaning her behind on an ATV on display.

"Oh, baby, I agree. That is surely the one that made the tread mark. I've been looking at all these gorgeous bikes on display."

"ATVs," the sales guy corrected.

"ATVs." She smirked. "None of them have anything like that on them."

"Right, these are replacement tires. The ones on display are what comes with the model ATV, brand and style. Mostly, they're set up for particular use—mud or sand. We sell a lot of both."

She nodded toward the glass door to a back room. "I saw a dirty one in there with those tires on it." She'd been nosing around the doorway, while the sales dude entertained Shea.

"The bikes in the back belong to customers who brought them in for repair or trade in, or they belong to the dealership for company use. They're not for customer viewing." He tried to steer Shea's attention back to the display. "Now these—"

She interrupted. "I want to look anyway. At least then, we can see what they might look like on our bikes."

"You're talking ATVs, right?" He frowned.

"She opened the door and walked into the back room uninvited. "Yeah, you know, quads."

He rushed to follow his errant customer. "Ma'am, we're really not supposed to bring visitors back here."

She turned to face him, flashing her badge. Shea pulled his out too.

The man's face blanched. "So, officers, what exactly do you need from me?"

Shea followed him into the room. "Actually, you've already been a significant help. We're looking to identify the tire that made this tread mark. We've nailed it down to the Dirt Digger. You have helped us determine the tire wasn't on a newly purchased machine but was a replacement tire for an existing quad. Now we need to figure out who owns such a tire."

"Man," the salesperson shook his head. "We have a lengthy list of customers who've purchased that one."

Reggie smiled at him. "We need you to make a printout of those purchasers."

"Well, I don't know." He hesitated. "That's privileged information.

Shea interjected, "We can get a warrant and be back in an hour. Are you going to make us do that? If so, I'll have the Sheriff to sit in front of your shop with his light on while we wait. That can't be good for business."

"Let me go talk to my manager." The dude sped out of the room before they could ask him anything else.

Reggie squatted. "This is the only quad in here with Dirt Digger tires. The machine parked in a back corner. It did not appear to have been moved recently and was blocked by other quads. "It's filthy." She pulled an evidence bag and tweezers from her pocket. Using the tweezers, she extracted several clumps of different looking types of dirt clods from several locations on the tires and ATV, placing them inside the bag. As she finished getting samples, the salesperson returned.

A taller, balding man in a rumpled, white shirt trailed him, a couple sheets of paper in hand. The salesperson stepped aside, and the taller man stuck a hand toward Reggie. "I understand you folks are law enforcement, and you need our help. We're pleased to be of any service we can be."

Reggie shook his hand. "Yes, I'm FBI Agent Reggie Montgomery." She flashed her badge then pointed toward Shea. "This is U. S. Marshal Shea Montgomery." Shea showed his badge.

"Good to meet you, Steve Morris here." He pushed the paperwork Reggie's direction, and she took it. "This is the list of customers who have purchased the Dirt Digger from us since we started selling it about fifteen months back."

She pointed to the bike behind her. "I noticed this one. Does it belong to someone on this list?"

Steve frowned. "Afraid not. That is a company quad. We keep it around for personal use and to help train new riders when they need lessons. It helps us keep 'em alive. You know?"

"It's muddy. When was it last used?" Shea glanced at the quad and back.

Steve thought a moment. "We haven't used it for lessons for quite some time. Usually, I'm the only one who uses it.

I've been too busy to ride myself lately. We do loan it to employees. Do you know who might've used it last?" He asked his salesman.

The guy shook his head. "It's been a while since anyone used it. A good month or so. I think Knapp might have taken it for a weekend. He keeps putting off cleaning it. Not been a rush."

"Knapp?" Reggie repeated the name.

The manager clarified, "Yes, our jack of all trades, part handy man, part delivery man. Nathan Knapp delivers ATVs when a buyer needs it. He cleans up around her, stocks, does lot maintenance, and washes quads as needed. He's a super guy, been here about twenty years or more. He's out on delivery now."

"We're going to need to talk with him. You can give us his contact information." She looked him in the eye.

"Of course." He spun around and walked out of the room. "I've got it at the front desk." The salesperson hightailed it to hidden quarters, as they had exited the maintenance room.

Shea and Reggie followed. Taking the paper with Nathan Knapp's address and phone number on it, they shook hands with the manager. "Thank you for your cooperation."

"Of course. Anytime. Anything more I can do?"

"Yes, should anyone borrow that machine again, please advise me." Reggie gave him her card."

"Will do." He looked puzzled as they exited.

CHAPTER 14

Sage stood in line to purchase fabric from a bolt she held in one arm, to sew new placemats and curtains for her dining area. The sewing shop was busy with several customers browsing around. A couple were in line at the front, and a clerk she didn't recognize was at the register checking them out. Two women in line in front of Sage meant they'd have to wait their turn. The lady being helped by the owner at the cutting table had several bolts of fabric to be cut to size. The table was large to accommodate two cutters at once, but today, there didn't appear to be anyone available to use the empty side. Luckily, the tall woman standing ramrod straight in front of her only had one piece, which appeared to have come from the Ends and Pieces section and a roll of lace. At least she wouldn't take forever to be served.

Ty was getting antsy as the five-year-old played and rambled around and round her heels. It was lunchtime, and he was looking forward to his burger meal, a treat and ice cream for dessert. She'd promised him lunch at Sadie's Royal Diner if he behaved himself at the fabric shop.

Shopping wasn't meant for small boys with energy she envied. Ty was usually well-mannered, but when he got 'hangry,' he sometimes required a heavy hand. He was the miracle child she'd always wanted, and it hurt her more than him when she had to correct him.

His foot slipped, as he danced around his mother. His tiny, gym-shoed foot contacted back of the lady's foot in front of Sage, landing squarely where her rolled-down, nylon stockings curled around her pure white ankle. The boy toppled onto his butt, looking up with a stunned gaze. He clearly knew he was in trouble. Fear radiated from his reddening face, that adorable face so like his father's; and his aqua-blue eyes filled with tears.

He glanced from his mother to the stranger who riled around toward him like she might knock him on top of his raven head with the heavy-looking, black purse hanging from her arm and looking like it had been used for a couple of decades. Not for knocking rambunctious children on the head, hopefully.

The middle-aged female didn't appear to spend much time outdoors, a blatant contrast to Sage's work-earned deep tan. Her grey-dark hair was in a fierce bun, with no strands daring to escape the tight knot. As she whirled toward Ty and Sage, her blanched face pinked. She glared and huffed as she tried to spit out her words. Her brow furrowed, and mouth pursed together.

"Aren't you the Sheriff's wife? One would think someone your age and stature would be able to control a small child."

Sage was taken aback more by the idea the woman seemed to have stepped out of a past era more than her words, though they stung. "Yes, I'm Sage Gordon. I apologize for my son. He gets antsy when he's in need of nourishment. It's past his lunchtime, and shopping certainly isn't his thing. Still yet, I do apologize. It won't happen again." She reached an arm and helped lift her son to his evil feet. "Ty, what do you say to the nice lady?"

Ty went into a pout, causing dimples he got from his daddy to show on his chirrup face. His voice was meek and filled with regret. "I'm sorry, ma'am. I won't bother you again."

Instead of listening to his apology, the snippy female spun as he stood, turning a cold backside on the two of them. Her message was clear. She wanted nothing to do with them, and she held distain for them both.

Sage shrugged it off and turned attention to her son. "Stay behind me, Ty. Mommy will be done in a few minutes, and we can go to lunch." She ushered him to her rear.

The cutter finished with the customer and motioned for the angry gal to step up. She ordered a length of her lace, and within a couple minutes, the pissed-off matron walked toward the register.

Sage moved to the table and placed her bolt down. Ty walked to stand between her and the table, watching over the top so he could see the work about to start.

Abby Deters, the store owner smiled sweetly, as she pulled Sage's fabric choice toward herself. "I'm so sorry for your wait, Sage. I'm short-handed today. One of my clerks called in sick. How much of this do you want?" She indicated the cloth.

"No problem. I'll take three yards, please."

"It didn't look like no problem. I'm sorry your wait ended in that confrontation. Don't mind her. It's not you. She's like that with everyone, been that way a long time." The fussy frowner was out of earshot.

Sage hated thinking badly of anyone. Surely, there was a reason for the woman's attitude. "Does that mean she acted differently at some point?" Everyone had redeeming qualities, though it was difficult to find them in some people.

Abby chuckled in a low tone. "Oh, yes. She was fine until her daughter died. Let's see, little Maggie was about my son's age. They were in the same class at Sunday School, so that would put her at about twenty-four-years old now, had she lived. Poor dear died during a tonsillectomy—drowned on her own blood. Sad. She was only six years old. Marianne has never been the same since she lost her."

Sage's heart went out to the stern, bitter female. It would kill Sage to lose Ty or Haley. Sage and her stepdaughter were as close as they would be if Haley had been born from her. "That would change a person."

"Yes, some cling to their faith. Others pull away. Marianne was a devout church member until Maggie died. She's never set foot in the building since losing her baby girl. The child is buried in the graveyard, though; and her parents keep it looking lovely—even got special permission from the congregation to plant a tree in Maggie's honor."

"That's nice. What church do you go to?"

"St. Joseph on Falmouth Street."

"Oh, I know it—beautiful church."

"Thank you. We love it. You should join us sometime for services." She handed Sage her fabric with a tag stapled to it with the cost. "Here you go. You ready to check out? We have some lovely new quilting cloth just in."

"Yes, thanks. I've neither the time or patience to quilt, and I need to get this little one something to eat." Ty was at the end of his shopping patience.

After paying for her purchases, she slid the bag over an arm and took Ty's hand with the other. Walking toward the door, it surprised her to run into her best friend.

Magnolia Blossoms

Reggie held the glass doors open, squatted and threw arms out. Ty ripped his hand from Sage's grasp and ran into Reggie's arms. Reggie wrapped him in a bear hug, stood on her navy pumps and whirled the boy around so his feet spanned out from their embrace. She sat the tyke on his feet.

"What's my best man doing here?" Reggie cocked her head, again squatting so she was eye-to eye with Ty.

It was a treat running into Sage and Ty. The little boy smelled of lilac soap and bubble gum, a delight to Reggie's nostrils. He looked exactly like Wyatt had at his age, as though Ty was his father's clone.

"Mommy and I are going to Sadie's for burgers and ice cream." He glanced at his mother as he tentatively said the last word. "Want to come?"

Sage's brow cricked above an eye. "We had an understanding about the ice cream. Right, Ty?"

"Yes, Mommy." Sadness only a small one can feel so intensely about losing something as minor as a scoop of ice cream, filtered his speech. He turned back to Reggie, whose hands had yet to release the little one, resting eagerly on his arms. "We're not allowed to eat ice cream, but we're still getting burgers. Can you come along, Aunt Reggie?"

She wasn't a blood relative, but Sage and Wyatt were among those few who made up Reggie's makeshift family. She was closer to them than her own, except for Grandpa, who had raised her. Her own parents were too busy with their careers to keep her close.

She released the boy regretfully and stood, straightening her navy pantsuit. "I'm sorry, Ty. I'd love to join you and your mommy, but I've got work to do. Thank you for the invitation. Maybe you, Mommy and I can go out to lunch another day."

As always, being around the child made her maternal clock moan and groan, reminding her time was running out. She and Shea had been trying but were yet unsuccessful at getting her pregnant, though practicing was incredible. It was true what they said. The older you were, the harder it was. Shea might be able to produce offspring into his nineties, given the little, blue pill. Reggie, on the other hand was forty. It might take a miracle for her to have a child of her own.

She gave Sage a hug and kiss on the cheek. Sage eyed her with a curious look. "Your job brings you to a fabric shop? Or did you see us inside and pop in to say hello?"

"No, I'm on the job, following a clue."

Sage nodded slowly, a knowing look on her face. After all these years, she knew better than to question Reggie about her work. Reggie had gone to Quantico soon as the roommates had graduated from Stanford.

"Okay, well, Ty and I will leave you to it. You and Shea need to come over for a meal soon."

"Yeah, we'd love that, if we ever get to take another break."

Sage knew well, living with Wyatt, how swamped Reggie, Shea, Wyatt and his team were with two major cases to solve.

"Bye, see you soon. Promise." Reggie waved as they left and headed toward the back.

A stop at the register sent her to the cutting table in search of the owner. There was no one there, but a lady carrying several bolts of fabric was walking along a back aisle. As Reggie approached her, the woman's apron came into view. She strolled to her side.

Magnolia Blossoms

"Hi, the lady at the register said you are the manager." She flipped her badge out for the woman to read. "I'm FBI Special Agent Reggie Montgomery."

"Yes, Abby Deters, owner, manager, bookkeeper, toilet scrubber . . . you name it. The buck stops with me." The pleasant woman chuckled. "What can I do for you Agent Montgomery?" She laid the bolts atop a stack on a table.

Reggie pulled out swatches of three floral prints, all of them dirty, and two showing signs of deterioration from age and the elements. She also held three small pieces of white lace. "I'm trying to learn about these samples. Would you have sold them?"

The woman reached for them. "May I touch them?"

"Yes, please." Reggie allowed her to take the pieces.

She laid them atop a stack of bolts. One by one, she examined them carefully. After several minutes, her head began to shake and lifted to look Reggie in the eye. "It's possible. These two," she pointed to the older ones. "they're petty old. I'm not sure if they came from my previous stock or not. Patterns come and go. Once a bolt is sold out, we can't be sure we can secure any more of the fabric, regardless how popular seller it might be. They could've come from my shop, or they could've come from one in another town. No way to tell, without a sku number. They do look familiar, but it could be because they look similar to others. The same goes for these laces." She touched the two oldest ones.

Reggie hadn't anticipated the parcels sparking immediate recognition, given their age.

"Okay, what about the third piece?" Remembering a nondescript piece of cloth from twelve or eighteen years back seemed unlikely. She was shooting slugs into the dark.

Abby perked up and smiled. "This is definitely from my shop. In fact, there's still a tiny piece on the Ends and Pieces table."

She strolled to one of the four tables nearby. All were piled high with thin bolts of remaining fabrics and appeared to be sorted per table based on the type of cloth. She pulled a cardboard with a strip of the fabric on it out from beneath several others and returned to where Reggie waited.

"Here you go. This is it." She laid the sample beside Reggie's swatches. Abby was correct. The pattern matched the newest victim's dress fabric. "There's almost a yard left."

"Great, I'll take it. I need the cardboard holder as well, showing the sku number and other data about it." She touched the fabric with a hand, as though hoping it would give her some clue as to who had held it previously and sewn a dress for a young teen about to be executed. The cloth refused to speak.

Abby broke the spell. "I'll get the lace. I still have some on the bolt." She sped past a couple aisles and on a side wall of shelving, selected a small trim holder, nearly full of white lace. "Here you go." Abby retuned to Reggie, her find in hand. Laying it beside the display of evidence, she smiled. "This is the one."

"That's great. I'll take the rest of that, but I need the holder too."

"What's this about, Agent Montgomery?"

"These swatches are evidence in a crime. I'm trying to learn who bought them. Do you have any way of tracking who bought the fabric and lace?"

Abby frowned. "I'm afraid not. I can track sales by sku and name if it was paid for by credit card, but a great many of our customers pay in cash."

Exactly what Reggie expected. Still shooting in the dark, but at least she'd hit one target. Maybe she'd get lucky again. "Okay, I need to purchase these items." Reggie pointed to the items Abby had place beside them, as she put the evidence back into the evidence bags, she'd carried them in and stuffed them into her pocket. "I need you to run the sku search and give me that list showing those who used their cards to pay—name and address, if that's available."

Abby's head rocked up and down. "It should be, but it's going to take me awhile." She strolled to the front, Reggie on her heels.

She spoke to clerk at the register. "Candy, I need you to take over the shop for a few minutes. I've got something important to do." Before Candy could argue, Abby had unlocked a side door and stepped into a cubical office. Reggie followed.

Abby took a seat behind a grey, metal, utilitarian desk with a Formica top. A ruler had been glued to the desktop. She indicated Reggie should sit in the guest chair across from her.

Abby stretched the leftover fabric along the ruler. "There's only three-fourths of a yard left. It's four dollars per yard. Since it's a remnant, it's marked down to two; so that's a dollar-seventy-five-cents." She stretched the lace out. "Five yards at two dollars a yard. That's ten dollars. We usually don't sell the boards or holders, but I understand why you want them. "Reggie handed her a ten and five from her pants pocket. "Here's fifteen dollars. That should cover it."

"Oh, honey, I was going to give it to you. It's a worthy cause, I'm sure." Abby shoved the money away.

"No, it's fine. The FBI will cover it. Take the money, please. I'll need a receipt."

Abby pulled a pad out of a desk drawer and scribbled on it then handed it to Reggie. "Will this work?"

Reggie read the receipt and pushed it into her back pants pocket. "Perfect."

Abby pulled a small bag from another drawer and put the pad away. Opening the bag, she stuffed the holder full of lace inside, folded the remnant and placed it there as well. She pushed the bag and the cardboard holder toward Reggie. Then she pulled out a small laptop. A few clicks later, three sheets of paper printed off the machine directly to Abby's back along a wall.

Abby perused the papers, stapled the top corner and handed them to Reggie. "Here you go. Each sale of the items shows whether the sale was cash or credit. The credit ones have the user's name and contact information in the visual with their signature."

Reggie scanned down the list. Several credit card purchases of the items coincided and were made in the last three months, giving her hope they might lead to something.

"That lace is my most popular seller." Abby grimaced. "The list of purchases is long. I had several holders of that same sku. This is the last one."

"Do you recall anyone in particular who purchased them together, say during the last month or two?"

"Honestly, I cut so much fabric, I couldn't swear to anything. I often know the types of things regular customers are looking for when they come in. Like your friend Sage, I saw you talking to her. Sage buys upscale, modern but cozy looking fabrics for household projects. She's got impeccable taste. Many of our shoppers are quilters, so they go through the cotton bolts like lightning. Something like the one you've got is super popular. Any one of a couple dozen people could've purchased it for that reason."

"Do many people sew clothing for their families?"

Abby shrugged. "Some but nothing like they used to. Fabric is more expensive. Sometimes it's cheaper to purchase an item off the rack."

"That can't be good for business."

"No, but there will always be young people wanting to learn the art of sewing. Women love quilting, and we sell tons of items for crafters. They've actually turned out to be the bulk of our shoppers these days."

Reggie took the list, her bag and the board then stood. "Thank you, Abby. You've been a great help. I won't keep you any longer. If you think of anything else that might be of help, let me know." She laid a card on Abby's desk. "I know my way out." She stood and opened the door.

Abby followed her out. "Anytime, Agent Montgomery. It's a pleasure to be of service."

The shop was brimming with customers. Four ladies stood in line to have their cuttings done. The clerk was busy clipping away. Others milled around looking at items near the cash register, clearly waiting for someone to approach that area.

Abby shouted across the tables filled with fabric. "Candy, I'm back. I'll ring the customer."

A relieved look came over Candy's flustered face. As Reggie walked out the door, the waiting customers rushed to get in line. Abby slipped behind the checkout table, and the door clanged shut behind Reggie.

Her phone rang. Pulling it from its pocket on her hip 'Mother' flashed on the screen. "Hey, Mom. How are you and Dad? What's going on?" Her mother rarely phoned, except for the occasional Sunday call.

Her mother's voice was unusually soft, for the get-it-done doctor. "Reggie, we're okay, but Grandpa. He had a heart attack on the golf course this morning. He's gone, honey."

Reggie felt the world around her slip away and disappear. The sidewalk seemed to vanish beneath her feet, and her heart sank.

The man had raised her. He'd been there when no one else would. He'd loved her. Fixed her boo boos. Taught her to shoot and how to drive. He was more father to her and more mother, than the tied-to-the-operating-room physicians who had birthed her. He couldn't be gone.

"No."

Magnolia Blossoms

CHAPTER 15

Sage and Reggie pulled into the parking lot behind the church. The graveyard butted up to one side of the holiday card-worthy, historical church and extended to woodland on one side, the parking lot and church on the other. A middle-aged man pushed a gas mower among the graves, while another worked a small machine used for digging a fresh grave—the one where Grandpa Morris would rest eternally beside Grandma. Reggie's eyes teared at the sight.

Sage placed a hand on her wrist and squeezed. "You ready to do this?"

Reggie sniffed and patted her eyes with the square, over-sized, red and white hanky Sage had given her when she'd broken down halfway there. Thank goodness Sage had offered to drive her. She was always prepared, and never failed to have a handkerchief ready in her back jean shorts pocket.

Reggie nodded. "Got to be. Might as well get it over."

She opened her door and hopped out of Sage's truck. Sage did the same and met her at the walkway, taking her hand and swinging it as they walked toward the rear entrance.

"Mom and Dad are flying in this evening. Shea went with me to the mortuary this morning to set up the viewing and arrange for them to pick the body up at the airport this afternoon.

Sage met her eyes. "It's good he spent his last days happily playing golf and reconnecting with his daughter and son-in-law, after all these years. He'd dedicated much of it raising their incredible daughter, and he remained devoted to you until the end. He and your grandmother worked hard all their lives. He deserved some rest and fun."

Reggie pushed back more tears and stretched her face as she blinked. "Yes, he and Grandma were everything to me. I'll always be grateful they were there for me, took me in, when Mom and Dad refused to settle down to a normal life."

Squeezing her hand, Sage chuckled. "Kiddo, there's no such thing as a normal life."

"Guess you're right, but trapsing around the globe, living in mud and shacks in third-world countries was not how a kid should grow up. I'm eternally appreciative my parents agreed to let me live with my grandparents when I reached school age."

"Your folks sure led an unusual life, globe-trotting with Doctors Without Borders and caring for those without basic resources. It takes a lot of bravery to live like that."

Reggie acknowledged with a nod. "It does, but it takes real guts to raise a child. I always felt my parents' chosen path was a bit indulgent on their part."

Sage opened the door. "I suppose some people have trouble giving up their dream . . . even for someone they love." She'd done it once then promised herself she'd never do it again.

Did Sage regret her choices? "Things turned out perfectly for you, though. You're happily doing what you dreamed of, running an organic farm; married and raising your son; and you have Hailey as a bonus." She followed Sage inside a slim hallway, open doors lining its sides.

"Speaking of my bonus child, Hailey called yesterday. She can't make it tomorrow. She and her new beau are on a teaching tour in Europe, and she is scheduled to talk at a conference in Switzerland tomorrow afternoon. She ordered flowers for Mr. Morris's grave and a swag for Mrs. Morris's also. She asked me to give her condolences."

"I appreciate that. That girl has grown into a marvelous adult. I understand from her last email that she's teaching Chemical Engineering at Stanford next semester. Her success is partly due to you, Sage. You've been a good mother to Wyatt's daughter. Someone needed to be. Her real mom is a wacko, if you ask me."

Sage snickered at the description. A tall, early-thirty-something man in a camo tee shirt and jeans stepped out of an office, swatting back stray strands of his sandy blonde hair. Work boots softened his steps as he extended a muscular arm and hand toward them. A brilliant smile bought out dimples on his pleasant face, and his eyes held what appeared to be genuine sympathy in them.

"I'm assuming you're Mrs. Montgomery, here to arrange Mr. Morris's tribute. My assistant told me you were coming. I'm Reverend Charlie Harman, Minister for St. Joseph Church."

"Yes," Reggie took his hand in a firm shake. Then he extended it to Sage. "This is my friend, Sage Gordon."

"Yes," he smiled. "Sage and I have met. Wyatt and I are old hunting buddies. When I moved to Sweetwater from Hazard, she helped me discover places to hunt and fish in the area and introduced me around to many of their friends. Wyatt speaks highly of you and your husband, Mrs. Montgomery."

"Yes, Wyatt and I are old friends, grew up together." Reggie and Sage followed the pastor into his office. He stepped behind an ancient, wooden desk, indicating with a wave that they take the two cushy guest chairs. "Most folks around here call me Chuck or Reverend Chuck."

"Thank you for seeing us today, Reverend Chuck. As I told your assistant, my grandparents were members of this church. Grandma is buried in the graveyard." Reggie nodded toward the window view.

The man who had been cutting grass when they arrived, was kneeling beneath a tree, facing a grave planted at its base. A monument with an angel statue atop it marked the grave. He appeared to be paying respects."

She turned attention back to the reverend. "Grandpa is to be buried by her side." She pushed the funeral home's card in front of him. "The wake is at the mortuary tomorrow afternoon from two to six. We'd like you to say a few words there at the end of the service and to officiate at the memorial service the next morning—here, if possible."

He linked hands atop the desk. "That would be fine. Does ten a.m. work for that?"

"It does." She passed him a copy of the obituary she and her mother had drafted. "This might help you determine what to say."

"Thank you. That's very helpful. I have been here for ten years and remember your grandfather well. He was a long-standing church member. I understand he and your grandmother raised you, while your parents worked overseas."

"They did. I lived with them from the age of five until I went away to college. We were close."

Magnolia Blossoms

"Well, I'm happy to help with the memorial service, and I'm pleased to meet you. I promise to say a few words over your grandpa that will make you and him proud."

Satisfied, she stood, followed by Sage. They shook hands once more with the minister.

Sage eyed Reggie. "You okay for a minute? I need to use the restroom before we leave. We've got another stop to make—the florist."

"Sure." Reggie smiled, and her friend disappeared out the door. Over her shoulder, she noticed the man in the graveyard had disappeared. The grave where he'd knelt was adorned with a bundle of flowers—white ones like those on the tree—a magnolia.

She'd been frustrated by the abundance of magnolia trees all over town, something she'd never paid attention to before. Many were ancient and new ones were sold by the co-op, the nursery just outside of town and even by the local florist. There was a big-box store that sold them in Bonnyville, as well as their town's nursery. She, Wyatt and Shea had visited every vendor selling them in a tri-county area and came up with nothing.

Reverend Chuck walked with Reggie toward the exit.

"Chuck, I noticed a maintenance man cutting grass in the graveyard."

"Yes, he takes exceptional care of our lot, though he's not our caretaker. He and his wife were once devout members. They no longer attend services, but he cares for the gravesites without pay. His daughter is buried there."

"Beneath the magnolia?"

His head tilted. "Yes, in fact. He got permission to plant it. Being a corner space there was no reason to refuse, especially considering all the work he donates. I don't know what we'd do without his help."

"Do you mind if I ask his name?" Something tickled in the back of her mind.

"Heavens no. It's Nathan Knapp. He and his wife Marianne lost little Maggie about twenty-four-years ago when she was five or six. I'm not sure which. I wasn't at this church that far back. Anyway, that's when the Knapps stopped attending church."

"Thank you, Reverend. I'll see you at the service, and I appreciate you doing this."

"It's my pleasure and an honor." He shook her hand, and as Sage returned, hers too.

Magnolia Blossoms

CHAPTER 16

Visitation was crowded with folks who had known Grandpa Morris when he was a vital part of the Sweetwater community. Reggie's friends Sage, Riley and Corrie kept close vigil near their friend, in case she needed a strong shoulder to lean on. Sage and Reggie had roomed in college and had been like sisters since.

Reggie had met Riley at a fraternity party and introduced her to Sage. The threesome had stayed close over the years, though Sage had married and moved to New York City with her first husband and taken a job with the FDA. Riley had returned home to northern Kentucky and opened her advertising company, The Power Agency, in Cincinnati. After a chance meeting and reuniting at Sage and Wyatt's wedding, Riley had married Levi Madison.

Reggie grew up with Wyatt, Corrie's older brother, Levi Madison, and tavern owner Justin Henderson. As Levi's kid sister, Corrie had tagged along, head-over-heels about Justin, who she married after leaving her philandering photographer husband in New York and returning to Sweetwater with her teenage daughter, Morgan.

These people had been there for Reggie most of her life, unlike her wayward parents, who had shipped her off to live with her grandparents. She'd grown close again with her parents, since their retirement, though they lived on the other side of the country.

Riley nodded her brunet bob toward the display of arrangements and casket in the front of the house of worship. I saw a huge spray from Shea's parents.

"Yes, they called yesterday. We had a video chat with them and my parents. They both had pressing commitments." *When did they not?* "They were appropriately sympathetic and said all the right words. Mom and Dad were pleased, but there was an edge to Shea's speech that told me he wasn't happy with them. He and his folks have a tenuous relationship, as you know. It's gotten better since they sold the business and have been traveling more. They act somehow softer, more relaxed about everything."

"Some people are difficult to understand, but I believe there's good in almost everyone." Sage was the eternal optimist. It came from her flowerchild background. Born in a hippie commune, her parents had moved to the suburbs to ensure Sage got a good education. Her love and peaceful attitude were right up there with her appreciation for nature.

"I sure hope you're right. I want to like Shea's mom and dad. Tolerance and polite conversation are all I can muster still yet. Three years of marriage hasn't changed that much. Shea understands. His feelings about them are a mixed jumble of pain, heartache, disappointment and bitterness, combined with loyalty of a son." Reggie wasn't sure who had been better off growing up, she or Shea.

"He's a good man, your Shea. How goes it with your folks?" Sage and Reggie milled around in the front of the church while mourners gathered and took their seats.

Magnolia Blossoms

Reggie glanced at the striking couple seated in the middle, front row. Her father's strong arm wrapped lovingly around his beautiful wife's petite, black, silk-clad shoulders. Her mother's greying curls hung attractively, just past her ears.

"We're good. They're still as in love with Shea as they've been since first meeting him." She gazed at her husband across the vestibule. He smiled back, clearly keeping one eye on his grieving wife in case she needed him. Her heart filled with gratitude for having found him.

"They're going home early day after tomorrow. Wouldn't want to linger too long in one place."

Sage gave her a knowing smile. "Well, there's no business for them to settle here. They're here for you now. I'm sure they appreciate knowing you're in fine hands with Shea."

Like she'd been in good hands with Grandma and Grandpa, when they'd dumped her off to live with them before flittering back to the remote jungles of Africa.

Reggie shrugged then glanced around her protective clan of friends. "You have always been here for me. I love Mom and Dad—always have, but you and Wyatt, Levi and Riley, and all the rest of my close friends in Sweetwater are my true family."

"Damn straight; we love you, gal." Corrie's long curls bounced as she reached to stroke an arm down Reggie's sleeve, through the filmy, black fabric.

"I know and appreciate it." She smiled at her gorgeous blonde friend. "I understood, even as a child, why they gave me up. It was out of love. They were good parents when I lived with them. They're caring and considerate now. At least since they're in the States again, we talk regularly and have gotten close again. Mom's grieving as much as I am, but she's used to leaning on Dad for comfort. We're all good."

Tall as Shea, Levi and Wyatt flanked Shea as they strode toward the gathering of women. Justin's limp from his artificial leg was barely perceptible as the deeply tanned, dark curled shorter man fast walked to keep up. Levi had tamed his unruly blonde locks for the day. They were a remarkable foursome, each different and unique.

Shea reached hands to take Reggie's "You doing okay, babe?" He waited for her nod. "Service is ready to start." He took her arm and led her to sit beside her parents. The gathering followed, filing into the pew behind them.

Mom smiled with teary eyes and slipped her hand around Reggie's. Reggie squeezed it with her fingers. Her father gave her a questioning gaze, and she nodded, telling him with her look she was alright.

The ceremony was brief and sweet, bringing tears to most eyes in the room. Her mom shuddered as she quietly wept into a tissue.

Afterward, mourners made a procession past the deceased and exited the building. Last to leave were Reggie's entourage, her parents, she and Shea.

As they passed by, she planted a finger kiss on her grandfather's cold cheek. He looked so much like he was merely napping. Tears flooded her eyes, knowing it would be the last time she saw him. She dabbed at moisture on her cheeks with a hanky.

Shea put a reassuring arm around her and led her outside. He kissed her cheek. "I'll be by your side in a few. The ladies have your back." He winked at the sisterly gathering—Sage, Corrie and Riley. The men went back inside.

It was a brief walk to the open gravesite at the adjoining graveyard. Parishioners had gathered for a last goodbye and stood in a ring around the empty cavity. Workers from the funeral home busily carried sprays of floral arrangements,

Magnolia Blossoms

placing them around the headstone which now held two names—Grandma's and Grandpa's.

Reverend Chuck strolled out of the back church exit followed by Grandpa Morris's casket, carried by Wyatt, Levi, Justin, Shea, and their friends, Moggie Larrs and Calvin Coldwater.

Cal was Jaiden's older brother and the retired Navy Seal trained racing horses for Levi at Mane Lane Farm. He had married Rose, Sage's partner and farmhand.

Moggie took early retirement as a wounded police officer, after being shot. He'd moved to Sweetwater when the group were mostly teenagers and had made a living as a farrier for many years. He was eventually hired on by the Farmers, now deceased, as a ranch manager.

Reggie had nearly had a fling with Moggie around the time of Corrie and Justin, and Levi and Riley's, double wedding. She'd pushed the notion of a one, or-at least two-night stand, aside when she'd learned her old pal, Dovie Farmer, was head over heels for Moggie and wanted a long-term relationship.

The men placed the casket on boards that had been erected over the gravesite. Then they came to stand beside their women. Shea took Reggie's trembling hand, and she smiled up into his soulful eyes.

Reverend Chuck said a few last words, then people began walking past. As each did, they plucked a flower from a bouquet and tossed it atop the floral spray-covered trunk that held Grandpa Morris. Reggie and Shea followed her mother and father.

She plucked a yellow rose from a bouquet and laid it gently across the top. "Bye, Pa. I'll always love and miss you."

Yellow was his favorite. Shea put a yellow carnation beside the rose then swept and arm around her waist, holding her securely as he walked her to the line of vehicles and helped her inside their limo. She appreciated how he was protective of her, as though she might crumble to the ground without its support—and she just might.

Reggie wrapped a palm around the diamond at her throat, needing comfort it provided. Comfort Shea provided. Her loving husband was more man than any other had ever proved to be. Having him by her side meant more to her than he'd ever know.

Their automobile led the others along the gravel path to leave the graveyard. As they turned to exit onto the street, they passed a corner gravesite, marked with a magnolia tree.

Magnolia Blossoms

CHAPTER 17

Reggie drove her parents to the Louisville airport. Her mother wrapped her elegantly clad arms around her daughter. "Are you sure you don't need us, dear? We can stay as long as you'd like."

Her handsome father stood behind her mother and gave Reggie a questioning look.

"No, thank, Mom, Dad. I'm fine. She's here, and my friends. You go on home."

"Okay, dear, if you say so. It won't be the same without Daddy in the next condo."

Her father took Reggie in his arms, and she soaked in his steady warmth, as she leaned her head on his suit coat. "No, it won't be. I've lost my best competitor and my best friend in the world." It was good her parents loved Grandpa so much.

"At least he got to spend his last years beating the daylights out of you on the course." Her mother chortled, half laughing, half crying.

"And I got to have him for his best years." Reggie tried to push tears down and give them a genuine smile. "I cannot believe he's gone. I guess I expected him to be eternal."

"He is, dear." Her mother touched Reggie's chest. "In here, he lives forever."

They shared another round of kisses and hugs, then The Doctor Casses walked toward the Security section, and Reggie headed back to Sweetwater.

Reggie spent a day milling about the house thinking of her loss. It made it worse. This wasn't how she handled problems. It didn't help to mull over them. Pain remained a dull throb in her heart, no matter what she did. By evening when Shea returned home to their temporary housing, she'd made up her mind.

"Hi, Baby. How are you doing?" Shea smiled as he entered.

"Stir-freaking-crazy. That's how I'm doing. I can't stand this. I need to work. There are to major cases on my plate. I don't have time to sit around licking my wounds. Spit doesn't solve a damned thing. Don't argue with me. I'm going back to work tomorrow." She handed him one of two icy beer bottles she'd prepared for her speech.

He snickered, opening his arms so she could enter them. She sat her bottle down on an end table and flung herself at her tall, sturdy man. Her legs wrapped around his waist, and her bare feet settled against his slight ass. She wrapped arms around his broad shoulders, and her curls hit his shoulder as she tilted her head to study him.

"I had no doubt you would be itching to get at it." He winked.

She kissed his rough, strong jaw all the way to his ear. Taking the lobe between her teeth, she nibbled and sucked, allowing hot breath to ooze out into his ear canal. It drove him crazy when she did that, and she loved the resulting protrusion of steel that met her bottom, where her privates rested against his jeans.

"Right now, I have another itch only you can scratch. And, lover boy, you sure know how to scratch it. Make me feel alive, Shea. Make me tingle from head to toe with the lifeforce."

He leaned toward the table and started to put his bottle beside hers. She shook her head and instead, picked hers up. "No, I'm thirsty. If you're not, you soon will be. Besides, the bottle could come in handy." She winked, as he carried her in a rush toward their bedroom, one hand on her butt, the other carrying his beer.

"You naughty girl. You might just need a spanking."

"You're right, Marshal. I've been wicked, and I'm about to be even more so."

Parents were always grieving, whether involved in the child's disappearance or not. Most times a parent, close friend or family member was responsible for abduction of a juvenile. No matter their emotional state, parents couldn't be ruled out.

The Moore's phones had been bugged to pick up any ransom call that might come. Ryan's direct company line had a tap on it in case a call from the culprit came through it. None had.

The family wasn't financially well off. They had no large stash of cash to be found. They saved a portion of his pay checks each month and used the remainder to live on. Neither parent came from money nor had prospect of inheriting any.

They'd interviewed Ryan and Twila Moore countless times so far, at their homes and at the press releases they'd done. Reggie decided to bring them to the Sheriff's office. Wyatt agreed and set it up. He met the Moores as they entered the Precinct. Some deputies were out in their cruisers or on calls. A few looked up from their desks at their arrival.

Wyatt extended a hand to Ryan, whose other arms was around Twila's shoulders. "Thank you for coming in today."

He ushered them toward a conference room. "This will make it easier for the three of us, Marshal Montgomery and Agent Montgomery and I, to talk with you at the same time."

It wasn't the sole reason. Reggie wanted to meet them in a formal, authoritative setting, out of their comfort zone. If they had anything to do with Blare's disappearance, they had yet to show signs of it. Parents were always suspect, but not enough to put them into an intimidating interrogation room.

The conference table was set with bottles of water, a bucket of ice, a carafe of coffee, cups and a bowl containing sealed containers of creamer and papers holding sweetener and sugar. Reggie and Shea sat along one side of the six-person table and stood as the group entered.

After greetings and hands shakes all around the couple sat across from Shea and Reggie. Wyatt took the head of the table. He pointed to the tray in the center. "Help yourselves."

Reggie broke the ice by taking a cup and handing one toward Twila. Ryan chose a cup, and Shea opened a water bottle. Reggie poured Twila's cup full, Ryan's and one for herself. "Wyatt, can I reach you something?"

"Water, please."

She handed him a bottle, and everyone settled into their seats.

Reggie took control, as it was her meeting. "We asked you here today to dig a bit deeper into what we already know and see what other clues to Blare's disappearance might surface."

Disappointment showed on the parents' faces. Ryan winced. "We'd hoped you might have news for us. We've braced ourselves for the worst but were hoping for good news."

"I'm sorry to say, we have yet to locate your daughter. Certain developments have occurred however, that lead us to believe Blare's being taken may have to do with another open case we've been working."

Twila's pretty face went from bleary eyes appearing ready to tear up to narrowed eyes and a grimace. "I don't understand. Is another child missing? I haven't heard anything about it . . . and we've stayed glued to the news." She cupped her mug, as though trying to soak up its warmth, though the room was already warmer than Reggie felt comfortable in. Wyatt liked it that way when speaking with perpetrators.

"Then you've heard we recently unearthed bodies on an abandoned farm outside of the city limits."

They nodded.

"We have no straightforward evidence yet, but we have strong suspicions Blare could've been abducted by the person who took those victims."

Twila sucked in a gush of air and turned to her husband, bleary-eyed. Sitting beside her, an arm swept around her shoulders, and his other hand took hers on the armchair.

With a sympathetic glimpse at his wife, he turned to Wyatt then Shea and landed on Reggie. "You're telling us a serial killer took our baby, and she's likely been murdered and buried somewhere?" Each word coming out of his mouth creaked out as though he was having to force speaking it.

Reggie pressed sympathy for them out of her mind and concentrated on doing her job—gathering information from whatever resources she would garner, to help find Blare Moore . . . hopefully alive. She needed to tread lightly, not to reveal key data about either case that had not been made public.

"You're partly right. We've learned things about the unearthed bodies, leading us to believe Blare may have been taken by the person who buried them. I know it's terrifying to consider; but if we're right, it could be a good thing."

Ryan's arm flew off his wife, and both hands slapped the table. "Blare is in the hands of a serial killer? There were three bodies. Right?" He waited for Reggie's quick nod of acknowledgment. As he spoke his voice grew louder and louder. "And that's supposed to be a good thing. How the hell do you figure?" By the time he finished, Ryan was shouting.

They'd anticipated this reaction. It was a normal one for a caring parent. Tears streamed unhindered down Twila's pretty face, and she heaved several thick breaths.

Magnolia Blossoms

Wyatt spun efficiently in his chair, opened a cabinet behind him and returned to face the table with his find. He pushed a flat, unopened, paper bag toward the mother. "You might need this."
He released it into her grip. "Breath into the bag. It will keep you from hyperventilating."

Twila did as instructed. Ryan's attention returned to his hysterical wife. A few minutes later Twila looked up and laid the bag beside her cooling coffee cup. "Thank you."

Reggie had sat waiting for calm to return, hands folded on the table's edge. Shea had sat silently with palms on thighs. The officers' expressions showed nothing but complete attention.

Reggie's head rocked side-to-side. "No problem. We understand how you must feel." After a nod from the couple, it seemed time to continue. "As I said, we believe Blare may've been taken by that person. If so, it's most likely she's alive and being well cared for."

Ryan glared as though staring at an alien creature. "How the hell could that be? That person killed and buried his victims."

All that had been released to the press was there were three bodies, and one was a recent burial. No condition. Nothing about appearance and dress when buried. Not even their ages. They needed to be cautious about what they told these two. Rumors pushed distortion of facts into the public; and the Sweetwater gossip mill was notorious, though well-meaning.

Reggie gave a single nod. "Yes, he did. Evidence shows he may've held them for awhile before killing them. While he did, they appear to have been well cared for. This gives us hope we could find Blare alive and well." She was silent while the parents turned to face each other and grasped hands together. "What we reveal to you today about that case is to stay with you. You only. Do not share with family, friends—no one. It could mean the difference between life and death for your daughter."

A small gasp flew from Twila's mouth, and her shoulders moved forward. "We won't say a word. We promise. Right?" She turned to Ryan.

He nodded. "Not a word."

Reggie had no hopes that would prove true, which was why she limited what she shared. "Good. I want you to go over again, exactly what transpired that morning. Start from when you woke." She sat back in her chair and folded hands in her lap. "Do you mind if we record this?"

"No, it's fine." Ryan spoke for them.

Shea talked into a recording device, explaining when, where and who was present and why. Then he sat back in his chair.

The room went silent for a few seconds. Ryan began the tale of what happened from waking to when he left for work. Twila bolstered herself with a long inhale and shoulder rock backward. She started from her point of view, what occurred until Ryan left. Then she repeated her story about what she and Blare did that morning to the point where they were outside, her sitting on the stoop watching Blare play with her dolls, as she waited for time to take her to the dentist.

Twila got to the phone ringing and having to run inside to get it. A light went on in Reggie's head. They had, like Twila, gone on the assumption it was a random sales call. "Tell me exactly what the man on the line said."

"It wasn't a man. It was a woman. She said she worked for Burton's Cleaners. They're local and have a good reputation, but I've never been on their website and didn't make an appointment. I clean my own carpets. The woman assured me the appointment request was made on their online scheduling system, asking them to confirm via telephone at ten-thirty a.m., before showing up for a one o'clock cleaning." Twila's frown appeared to be holding back tears.

Ryan released his wife and leaned forward. "What are you getting at?"

Reggie gave him what she hoped was a reassuring look. "I'm simply searching for clarity. This is the first we've heard of the actual conversation between Twila and the caller. It could be a simple mistake, or like you said a sales ploy to get your business. Or, one of your neighbors might've made an appointment and gave the wrong address. It could've been a prank by some teenagers."

Or someone scheduled the appointment as a distraction, to keep Twila busy while they nabbed her daughter.

A woman.

"We will follow up with the cleaning company." Reggie mentally noted to call Sage, the area's liaison to the Kentucky State Cyber Crime Unit in Louisville. After they got the goods from the business, assuming it wasn't a sales gimmick, there should be an IP address linked to the data plugged into the appointment request online. It was beginning to sound like the phone call wasn't a coincidence after all.

Reggie's feeling about this meeting with the parents hadn't been wrong. An itch had been telling her they'd missed something of key importance. *This might be it.*

It might not. She pushed Twila forward, and ensured the mother repeated everything they'd previously heard about what happened next. One couldn't be too thorough.

Nothing else stood out as a dangling end. Exhausting the story and the Moore's, Reggie stood. Shea, Wyatt, Ryan and Twila followed suit. Reggie extended hands to the couple and accepted limp but grateful shakes and thanks.

Wyatt walked to the door and waved a hand. Jaiden Coldwater perked her dark head into the room. Recalcitrant curls had been tamed into a thick bun at the top of her petite head. "Mr. and Mrs. Moore, thank you for coming today. This has been a productive meeting. Deputy Coldwater will show you out." He waved a hand toward Jaiden.

Wyatt and Shea shook hands with the couple, and they followed Jaiden down the hallway to the bullpen then out massive wooden double doors. Wyatt clicked his office door shut and took his seat. "Well, what do you think?" Long fingers clasped together behind his head, and he leaned back in his chair.

Shea chewed the side of his lip. "Same thing we've heard over and over, but this phone call is curious. Could be something."

Reggie smiled. "Agreed. It's the only thing they told us we haven't explored further. She'd acted like it was just a sales call. We know how many of those we all get every day. Lots of folks don't even answer their phones unless they recognize the caller."

Shea snickered grimly. "Yeah, the No Call List is a joke these days."

"Still, I feel like a dumbass, for not pushing her harder earlier on this point." She gritted her teeth.

"Let's check out the cleaners in person. It's the best lead we've got so far." Shea stood, followed by the others. Wyatt flipped his hat on his head.

Wyatt held the glass door open for Reggie to enter Burton's Cleaners. He stepped inside and allowed Shea to grab the door and enter behind him. The small lobby tile floor and a couple of waiting chairs along one wall faced a

Magnolia Blossoms

clerk's table with a cash register on it. A half wall separated the front entryway from the dry cleaners' operation area where they cleaned everything from upholstery to wedding gowns. A pert, middle-aged, petite woman with a belly bump and thick hips walked around the wall to greet them with a broad smile on her plump face. She wore a pink smock over a pair of jeans, and sneakers completed her outfit. Curly, greying brown hair was pulled into a topknot.

"Sheriff Gordon, how nice to see you. That pretty wife of yours get tired of cleaning your uniforms, or do you need to schedule the office floors to be shampooed again?"

Wyatt smiled and stuck thumbs into his utility belt. "No Sara, I'm not here today for cleaning. I've brought along some colleagues. We're hoping you can help us with some information." Wyatt waved toward Reggie and Shae. "This is Deputy Shea and Special Agent Reggie Montgomery. Reggie, Shea, this is Sara Burton. She's the backbone of this operation, though her husband takes most of the credit. We're working on the Blare Moore disappearance case." Reggie and Shea flipped their badges toward her then put them away.

"Heavens, that poor child. I sure hope you find her soon. Her parents must be frantic."

Reggie stepped forward. "They are, and we're hoping you can help us find her."

Sara grimaced, looking to the side and back, confusion in her eyes. "I'd love to help you but have no clue how I might do that."

Reggie placed a card on the desktop. Shea did the same then stood back, leaving Reggie in charge. "We've learned that Twila Moore received a phone call from your company that morning. She went inside to grab her call. When she returned, Blare was gone."

"Well," Sara appeared to be thinking about that, glaring at the tabletop. "If that's the case, I would've made the call.

I schedule appointments for our cleaners, and I make calls to clients who fail after a week of cleaning, to pick up their goods. Let me check. What day was that?"

Wyatt gave her the date. She pulled a book out from behind the counter and laid it on the top. Flipping a few sheets, she landed on that date's page. "I print out the online schedules for the dates as they're updated." She pointed to another page next to that one. "This is my schedule for calling on late pickups. The other is the carpet and drapery cleaning schedule. Let's see. There was an online scheduled appointment for that afternoon at one p.m. The comments section says to call before arrival to confirm, and requested the call at ten a.m. I always call first anyway, in case they forget the appointment, have special needs or to remind them to put pets up. This is where I checked after making the call. I put a line through the appointment, showing it cancelled. It was either a mistake, or someone put in the wrong phone number or address. Cases like that, all I can do is wait and see if they call back to reschedule."

"You don't try to find out who the appointment was meant for?" Shea inquired.

Sara shook her head. "Not worth the time it would take, and it would be like taking a pot shot in the dark."

"Understandable," Wyatt added.

"So, Sara, do you delete the online appointment? Or is that still in your system?" Reggie needed more information.

"I can't be at the computer all the time, with customers in and out of the store all day. That's why I work from a printout. I make the calls here in the front or at the desk in back, between customers. When I have a few minutes, or in the evenings at home, I go into the system and mark the appointments as cancelled or rescheduled. My husband Harvey does most of the in-home cleaning, along with another cleaner, Joe Mason. When they complete a job, they enter it into their laptops on site. That generates an invoice. They print one for the client on site and mark it whether paid or not. That goes into our system for our accountant to manage our income. He sends out invoices to those not paid at time of service. This only happens for corporate jobs where they might have a specific department issuing payment for work. Most folks pay either by check, cash or credit card at completion."

Reggie sought clarity, pointing at the paperwork. "So, you mark those who reschedule and arrange rescheduling. The ones, like this one, that are cancelled, are left marked cancelled in the system. I see there's no email given by the client on this request."

"Exactly. Yes, we request an email address as well as phone number, in case something like this happens. Lots of folks are private about that, not wanting a lot of sales spam coming into their inboxes. You know how it is." Sara smiled up into Reggie's eyes.

"Certainly. I'm the same way." She smiled at the pleasant woman.

"I'll bet you are, being an FBI agent and all."

Reggie stood up straight, after being bent over the countertop, and stretched her back. "Sara, we're going to be a bit more bother. We're going to need to investigate this entry in your system. Would you or Harvey have an issue with our sending an expert to check it out?" If they balked, they had enough evidence this could be pertinent to the case to get a warrant to search for the IP address.

"Absolutely, you send them right over. That child's life could be at stake. It's killing me knowing my phone call could've played a part in her disappearance."

"Great. Don't change anything, especially around this entry. I'll ask Sage Gordon to look at your system today. She's the cyber expert for the Sheriff's Department."

"Oh, I know Sage. She's Wyatt's wife, the organic farmer." Sara looked pleased to have a friendly face be the contact she'd have to spend the afternoon with.

They returned to the cruiser. From the front passenger seat, Reggie called Sage. After initial greetings, Reggie explained the situation. "Sage, I know you have a lot on your plate. I need you to drop whatever you're doing and get on this immediately."

"No problem. I agreed to do just that and step into my role as needed." Sage had the habit of getting involved in Wyatt's cases, and even crimes he didn't know about yet, on her own.

Wyatt had finally decided to use her lust for crime solving and her technical knowledge and skills to the betterment of all. He'd hoped her assignment as Liaison would keep her out of harm's way, since she had proved to be a danger magnet. It was a part-time position on an as-needed basis. She'd not disappointed in the past and had helped put many a bad guy behind bars.

"Sage, I need you to go through that company's system. Get me an IP address for the contact who scheduled that appointment for the Moores. Once you get the IP, trace it to the owner, and hopefully the address and contact information. With luck, the owner will be the person we're looking for. Or they can lead us to whomever snatched that little girl and on to Blare Moore's whereabouts."

"You think the kidnapper, or an accomplice, made the appointment hoping to distract Mrs. Moore long enough so they could take Blare? I'm on it. Rose will be fine tending Ty and taking care of the farm. If she needs help with him, she can get Morgan to babysit."

A harumph came from the front seat, Wyatt's direction, as he drove them toward his office.

"Sage, by no means are you to investigate anything you find. You are to search the system and report findings immediately to Reggie, Shea and me. Understand?"

A pang of guilt hit Reggie. Sage had a habit of stumbling into dangerous situations without Reggie's help. She sure didn't need to be pointed toward it.

"Understood. Tell my sweet man, I will not seek out the owner of the IP address on my own. I'll provide you the data. You law dogs can go get the SOB—and save the girl. Pleeease, find the girl."

Reggie understood. It ached for parents like Sage and Wyatt, with small ones of their own, knowing a kidnapper of children was loose in Sweetwater.

Reggie hit the button to disconnect the conference call she and Shea had been on with Carla Orson. Carla, from NCMEC, National Center for Missing and Exploited Children, had met with the three victim's families and advised them of when they might be able to secure their children's remains. Shea's chair groaned as he leaned back and stretched.

Shea touched her hand across the small table between their desks in the office they'd set up five years ago—the crazy day they'd met. It was located at one end of a nondescript strip mall with a pretext of being an insurance agency. They had two exits, one to the shared hallway used by other tenants, and the other to the back private parking lot where they kept a spare vehicle handy and parked their rides. The one-room office had nothing more than a couple of plain, military-style metal desks, a worktable between them and a printer table behind them. The back wall held a corkboard with pictures of missing kids from across the tri-state area—Kentucky, Indiana and Ohio. The only other conveniences were a restroom and a supply room which housed office supplies and mostly weapons.

"Babe, I'm have to go out of town for a day or so. A Federal Judge needs escorting to and from court on a major trial."

Knowing he couldn't divulge more than that, even where he was going, she didn't ask. "When are you leaving?"

"Five a.m. tomorrow."

With lips pursed together, she nodded. "Be careful and come back safe."

"You know it, babe. Always." He squeezed her hand and released it. "I'm starved. Let's grab pizza and head home." Darkness had fallen, and as usual, they'd worked well into the evening.

Reggie's phone rang. The screen showed a photo of Sage with the time stamped on her face saying it was nine-thirty. No wonder she was bushed.

"Hi Sage, you're on speaker with me and Shea. What did you learn?"

"The IP was for a library computer." Sage's New Yorker turned Southern twang combination was adorable. She'd acclimated well to the south. "So, I went to the library. The time stamp on the communication allowed me to figure out which computer was used out of the ten available. The library doesn't require people sign anything at the desk for computer usage. Patrons simply sign on to any computer not in use at the time."

"Don't they require a card to use library resources?" Shea inquired.

"Good thinking, Marshal." Sage chuckled. "They do indeed. It's not totally anonymous. The user must slide their card into a slot or key their membership number into a screen to start the computer. Then they're able to type, print, use any software or go into a private email address or on the internet."

Reggie saw where she was going. A jolt of excitement shot through her veins. "So, you were able to determine the identity of the user by their library membership number."

"Exactly."

"Stop stalling. Get on with it, Sage. You're killing me."

CHAPTER 18

Reggie sat at her lonely breakfast table, computer at her side. Might as well investigate where Sage left off.

She pulled up the death certificate for Maggie Knapp. *Death by asphyxiation due to pneumonia caused by blood flooding the lungs during extraction of the tonsils.* Maggie had died as the shop owner had told Sage. Unfortunately, it had happened many times in the past, but more often to adults. Medical science had improved in the decades since, and this sort of thing rarely happened in today's world. Medicine had come a long way in the last twenty-four years. Surgeons had more effective ways to stop a patient from bleeding out on the operating table now.

She switched to the database of missing children. Reviewing listings of the three recently unearthed bodies, she finished her third cup of coffee. Something caught her attention. The oldest girl went missing not long after Maggie's death. That victim died six years later at the hand of their serial killer.

Did Maggie's dying have anything to do with it? Was someone in Maggie's family abducting the children, holding them six years and then killing and replacing them with a new child? It was a far-fetched idea, but she'd seen worse in her career with the FBI.

She had to find out, and it couldn't wait.

Reggie had grown used to having Shea as her partner. She was edgy about going it alone. Her team was busy following other leads. Most of them were outside the area anyway. Wyatt was on a hit-and-run call with Jaiden and Leo. There was no one else to partner up with.

She couldn't wait. Enough time had elapsed. She needed to exhaust this lead or find that kid, one or the other.

It had been a long time since Reggie had worked alone, but she had good experience at it. She'd worked solo for many years before meeting Mr. Tall, Lanky, By The Book But Sexier Than Hell. Reggie was more than capable of checking out a lead alone. Chances were she'd simply get enough data out of a visit to Maggie's parents to cross off another blind lead.

Reggie eyed the meticulously kept lawn surrounding a mid-sized brick ranch. The house was well-cared for on a quiet country lane.

She'd expected it to be tended and wasn't surprised to see a couple of magnolia trees growing in back. Apparently, the Knapps liked them. They'd planted one at the graveyard behind little Maggie's headstone.

She straightened her navy blazer, as she knocked on Marianne and Nathan Knapp's front door. A middle-aged woman with ramrod straight posture, wearing a shift with nylon stockings rolled around her ankles and feet in sturdy black shoes, answered the door. She recognized her as the stern woman who had passed her as she exited, and Reggie had entered the fabric shop the day she met Sage and Ty there.

"Yes?" Her greeting bore no welcome but may've been tinted with a layer of irritation.

"Mrs. Knapp?"

"Yes." Not much help there.

Reggie took a step toward her, though the screen door separated them; and she'd yet to be invited in. "FBI Special Agent Reggie Montgomery." She flipped her badge open. "I need to speak with you about a pressing issue. May I come in?"

It appeared Mrs. Knapp wasn't interested and might be trying to come up with an excuse to refuse. She finally pursed her lips and held the door open. "If you must."

"Thank you. I appreciate your time. I realize I showed up unannounced."

The stiff woman flipped a hand toward a sofa. "Might as well sit, though I can't imagine what you want with me."

Reggie took a seat on the couch. "I'm working on a couple of cases in the area. I'm hoping you might have seen or heard something that could help us solve them. I'm canvassing several neighborhoods." She had a hard time thinking of one she hadn't already canvassed. The unending search for Blare had proved to be one disappointment after another.

"Makes no sense to me. What do you want to know?" She stood tall across from where Reggie sat, hands folded in front of her.

"Well, I'm sure you've heard of the missing child case and the bodies that were recently discovered on an abandoned piece of property nearby."

A solum nod. "I'm not a hermit. Of course, I have. What about them?"

"I'm working both cases. I was actually hoping to be able to talk with you and your husband. Is he home?"

"He's working. Should be here for lunch any time now." No expression. "What do you want with us?"

"Well, since you aren't sure when he'll return, I'll start with you. I understand you're a patron of the local library."

The woman blinked a couple times without changing her stern expression. "I enjoy reading, and the Sweetwater Library has a broad selection of biographies."

"And the computers, do you use them?"

Her nostrils spread as she sucked in oxygen. "Occasionally. We don't have one of our own. I sometimes email my sister from the library." Her arms crossed in front of her.

"Yes, and you search the internet as well."

A brow shot up. "What of it? I wasn't aware the FBI cared who uses the internet. If you've checked my computer usage, you've invaded my personal privacy. I'll have to speak with my attorney about that."

"We don't normally care, Mrs. Knapp. What we do care about is solving crimes. We believe you can provide information that can help do that."

"Doubtful. I don't pay attention to others using library access when I'm there. I mind my own business, and I'd appreciate it if others would do the same." Her lips lightened as she pursed them.

"I'm not interested in your take on other library users. I'm interested in your usage of a library computer on September 31, this year."

Marianne shrugged a shoulder. "I can't recall what date I last used that facility."

"It was definitely September 31. You logged into a computer with your library membership card and were filmed on security cameras that morning."

Magnolia Blossoms

"What of it?" Her brows rose with a snort, eyes shooting to the side and back to stare at the coffee table. "I have a library card. Computer usage is part of the service they provide. I have every right to use them."

"Yes, you do. I'm not contesting that." Clearly, she had made Marianne sufficiently nervous and thrown her off her pissed-off persona game. She was in defense mode. Now Reggie wanted her to stew a few minutes. "I'm sorry. I've been out running all morning. I haven't been anywhere near a restroom. Would you mind if I used your facilities?"

Marianne's head shook at the off-the-wall request. She pointed to the next room. "It's off the dining room, first door to the left. Help yourself. I just cleaned in there." The implication was clear. She'd have to clean again after Reggie used the room.

Reggie walked into the neatly furnished dining room. A crocheted, lacy tablecloth covered an antique table, surrounded by six chairs with brocade covered cushions. A matching antique buffet held vintage, floral print China and sparkling glassware. Lace curtains matched the tabletop pattern hanging between thick, dark drapes on a double window to the back. Bedrooms were down a hallway to the right. The kitchen was open and off the left through the second doorway beside the bathroom.

Reggie must've interrupted Marianne's sewing. A portable sewing machine had been set up on one end of the table. A section of pink, floral print laid in front of it. Pink thread of the same shade had been assembled on the machine, and a strand of familiar looking white lace laid atop a pair of white girl's socks.

Reggie glanced inside the small kitchen. It was retro-1970's with aqua and black vinyl walls halfway up. Black and white, block flooring shone, proving miraculous care and heavy wax can ensure a long life to vinyl tile. Appliances were white and aged but immaculate. Ruffly, white curtains framed a window above a wide, porcelain sink top. It's white, metal cabinets and those hanging on walls were old but appeared to have been well-kept and freshly painted. It was a pleasant, sunny room.

She stepped into the bathroom and closed the solid, wood door. A white, claw-footed tub showed pitting from age but shinned as though defying its age. Two towels hung from a rack. Walls were freshly painted to match the pink sink and toilet. All were spotless.

She eased the mirrored door, holding it tightly go avoid a creaking noise, as she opened it. The tiny, in-wall, medicine cabinet was orderly, holding nothing more interesting than a couple of toothbrushes, toothpaste, a razor and bottle of shaving cream, a box of bandages and a bottle of aspirin. Nothing for a child.

This could be another dead end.

Or not. Either way, she'd find the girl or cross off another lead. She was here. Marianne was properly primed. Marianne's sewing project was curious. *Might as well see it through.*

She walked back into the living room. Marianne was seated on the sofa. She indicated Reggie should take the chair opposite her, facing the outside, front wall and entrance.

Reggie smiled as she made herself comfortable. She slid her phone out of her blazer pocket and held it in hand. Her other fingered the diamond at her neck, wishing Shea was with her.

"Are you a quilter, Mrs. Knapp?"

"Quilter? Heavens no. I have no time for such nonsense. Why would you ask?"

Reggie shrugged. "I noticed the fabric beside your sewing machine. It looks like cotton, which is a standard for quilters. I'm curious about the lace and socks sitting beside the fabric. They don't look large enough for you."

Magnolia Blossoms

When it was clear Mrs. Knapp had no intention of explaining further than her previous answer, Reggie got down to business. "Mrs. Knapp, the morning Blare Moore disappeared, her mother, Twila Moore, received a phone call from a carpet cleaner."

Sitting stiffly with hands on knees, Marianne blustered, "What does this have to do with me? I don't clean carpets, and I never called that woman. I don't even know her."

"I get that, Mrs. Knapp. However, the carpet cleaner's online records show they had an appointment to clean Twila Moore's floors that afternoon."

"For goodness's sake, I have things to do. You're wasting my time. I have no knowledge of, nor do I care about Mrs. Moore's cleaning habits."

Reggie's gut to told her it was working, and that getting Marianne frustrated would play to her advantage. "I believe you may have. As I was saying, someone made an appointment for one p.m. that day. The request online asked the cleaning company to call ahead of time."

"I would think they would do that anyway. It sounds like good customer service if you ask me." Her nose shot up.

"Yes, well, it was specifically asked that they call at ten a.m. precisely. The child had a dental appointment. The mother had been watching her play outside in the meantime. They were preparing to leave when the phone rang. Mrs. Moore ran inside to get her phone. The caller kept her busy for a few minutes, in which time her daughter vanished."

"I suggest you should be talking with that caller, not wasting my time."

"I'm getting to that."

"Well then, how about you get on with it?" She quirked a brow, glaring.

"Yes, well, we have proof you made that appointment."

The first expression change came from Marianne. She appeared to realize she'd been found out. Her face softened, as what appeared to be resolution melted her stern exterior. She huffed out a breath, glancing to the side and down, as though gauging her next move.

Reggie slid her phone between the seat cushion and arm of her chair, as she felt the presence of another in the room. Someone moved swiftly behind her. Before she could spin, a prick burned the side of her neck. Hot lava was forced into her jugular.

As her eyes closed, all she could think of was her husband's name.

Shea.

Magnolia Blossoms

CHAPTER 19

Reggie awoke with a massive headache. Her neck was sore. Hands were bound in behind. Ankles were tied and linked to her wrist bindings behind her back. Propped against corner walls on a floor that felt like cement covered with carpeting.

The room was quiet, which was a blessing to her major hangover. She stretched her neck to feel it. Her chain was still around her neck.

Groggily she blinked, trying to get her eyes to focus. Her mouth felt like it was coated with thick, dry slime.

Where was she, and how did she end up here?

Slowly it came back to her. She'd been talking with Marianne Knapp and waiting for Nathan to arrive home for lunch. Someone had stabbed her with a syringe, clearly with some type of drug in it. Whatever it was, she'd gone out like hooker on a Saturday night.

Nathan must've come home while she was in the restroom. He'd been cagey about it. She hadn't heard a sound. That must've been why Marianne had forced her to sit in a different location. She'd played right into their hands. What a fool!

What were they going to do with her now?

Silence was broken by a soft shuffle. She wasn't alone.

She gazed around the dimly lit room. Walls were a soft pink. A twin bed was covered with a pink bedspread trimmed in ruffles. No windows. Stuffed animals decorated the bed. A short, white vanity sat along one wall. Various cartoon characters were painted on another wall-Cinderella, Snow White and the Seven Dwarfs. This was a child's room.

Again, the soft shuffling noise; and a tiny head popped up over the bed. Catching a glimpse of her opened eyes, the child popped back down, hiding behind the furniture.

"Hi, it's ok. I'm not going to hurt you. I couldn't anyway. I'm all bound up."

"I know." She rose again, her full face visible now—Blare Moore. "I watched them tie you."

"I must look like a turkey on Thanksgiving morning."

That elicited a small giggle.

"Blare, I know who you are. My name is Reggie. I'm an FBI agent. I've been trying to find you. Are you okay?"

"Yeah," a meek reply came.

"I'm going to figure out how to get us out of here, Blare. Understand. Your parents are sick with worry about you. You need to trust me. I will get you back to them."

"They said Mommy and Daddy were dead, and they're going to take care of me now. I don't see how you think you're going to be any help. You're as stuck as me." She stood to full height, wearing a yellow, floral dress. Her hair had ben put into pigtails, and she clutched a stuffed bunny in her arms.

"That's a temporary situation. There are other officers collaborating with me. They'll find us, or I'll get us out of here somehow."

Yeah, sure. She'd forgotten to tell Wyatt where she was heading. So much for going it alone. Shea's face flashed through her mind, and tears started to form. She pushed them back.

No time.

"Listen, Blare, your parents are alive. These people lied to you. Your mommy and daddy know I'm looking for you. I promise. I'll get you home to them." She didn't yet know how, but she meant what she said.

Blare's eyes teared up. "I miss my mommy and daddy. That woman told me they were dead and she's my new mommy."

The expected story. "Well, Blare, they're not. These people are liars. How many are there?"

"Just him and her—my new mommy and daddy." She sniffed.

"Blare, they've taken you without your parent's consent. Your mom and dad want you back. They love you. Understand?"

"Uh, huh. I love them too." Several sniffles. "I want to go home."

"Okay, then. I need your help. Blare, can you come around and untie me? The knots feel tight, but maybe you can bring something we can use to pry them loose."

"No, I can't." Her head shook.

"It's okay, they're gone for now. I won't let them hurt you for helping me. They're not mad at you for me being here. They're just mad at me. I need to get loose and find a way to get us out of here before they come back."

"I can't."

"Sure, you can. You're a big, smart girl. You can do it." She understood the child's fear. She'd been through trauma. Blare needed encouragement.

Blare walked to the foot of the bed to stand between it and the dresser. Then she stepped past to stick her foot out as far as she could.

"No. See. I really can't. My foot has this metal thingy around it, and it's chained to the foot of the bed. I can only walk to the dresser and around the end of the bed. I can get in and out of the bed and play on this side. That's as far as I can go." She cried harder now.

Damn.

Doc said something about strange calcium buildup on the victims' ankles. Being chained to a bed for six years would do that.

No wonder.

These sick bastards were going to pay.

This poor baby must be terrified. She needed her help and didn't want to scare Blare any more than she already was.

"It's okay, Sweetie. I'll figure something out. Don't you worry."

Sage rang Wyatt, "Hi, Babe. How's it going?"

"Slow. How about you and our boy? Glad to be back at the farm?"

"Yeah, and Ty's glad too. He's playing with the goats while Rose and I make goat cheese. We're keeping an eye on his through the window."

Magnolia Blossoms

"Give my boy a hug."

"Will do. Say, why don't you invite Reggie to dinner tonight? She's alone, with Shea out of the country for a couple days."

"I'll give her a call. I haven't seen her all day." It was nearing four p.m. Reggie and Wyatt usually updated each other before calling it a day. They could do it over dinner if she was available to come over. Sage loved feeding people.

"Great, thanks, Babe. See you later." The line went dead.

Wyatt tried Reggie's phone. No answer. He wandered into the bullpen. Leo and Jaiden were the only deputies working at their desks. "Either of you talk with Reggie today?"

Leo's blonde head peeped up. "Not me."

Jaiden's eyes squinted. "I've called her a couple times this afternoon but got nothing. I left her a voice mail. I wanted to chat about my findings working with Blare Moore's dentist. I'm writing the report up now, and I was going to go over it with you soon as I finished."

He propped his butt on a file cabinet. "So, let's do it now. You can read her in later, or I can. I tried to reach her to invite her to dinner. She didn't answer my call either. How many times did you call?"

Jaiden glanced to the side as though thinking. "I called around ten, then again approximately twelve-thirty and again around two. It's not like her to be out of pocket for so long."

"No, it's definitely not. Well, give me the scoop on the dental connection."

Jaiden gazed at her notes a few times as she informed him and Leo of her learnings. "The appointment was made a month prior by Twila Moore to see Dr. Simpson at eleven a.m. that morning. The staff consists of three women, Marsha Baily, Cora Dane, Abigail Karney and then there's

Barry Simpson, the dentist. Marsha makes appointments, takes calls, takes payments at time of appointment and takes care of paperwork. Cora is their in-house accountant. Abigail is the dental assistant. Marsha recalls making the appointment, and they have an automatic call system that reminds patients of their scheduled time a couple days prior to them coming in. Appointments are posted on a board in Simpson's office. Anyone working there has access to the board, as his door is never locked."

"Nothing on the employees linking to Blare's disappearance.

"Not a dadburn thing." She shook her head, looking disappointed.

"No one else has access to the facility?" He was looking for a needle in a haybale.

"Only the housekeeper. She's an old church friend of Simpsons. Her name is Marianne Knapp, and she comes in on Thursday evenings, after the staff has gone home. She has her own key."

"Knapp? That name sounds familiar." Wyatt frowned.

CHAPTER 20

"Too bad you couldn't reach Reggie. I tried her after I gave Ty a bath this evening. No answer. That's not good." Sage sat down at the dinner table, Ty to one side wolfing down his beef stew and Wyatt at the other, waiting patiently for her to join him.

"Yeah, I tried several times. So did Jaiden. This is concerning, especially with Shea out of town." Wyatt took a bite and smiled. "Delicious. Too bad she's missing out."

"Thanks, Babe." She'd lost her appetite but needed nourishment after the long day working at the farm. She took a small bite of the savory dish, one of her favorites. Laying down her spoon, she stared at Wyatt. "I'll try her again after we eat. If I don't reach her, I'm texting Shea. I'm sure he knows what's up with her."

"Good idea."

After they finished, Sage put the food away and cleaned up. In the living room, Wyatt helped Ty with his new NO FEAR Learning and Activity Book. Dishes done, Sage pulled her cell out and rang her best friend.

Again, no answer.

She wrote a brief note to Shea. *"No word from Reggie today. Not answering phone. What's up with her?"*

Her text garnered a quick response. *"Me either. No answer. No text. Concerned?"*

She texted. *"Yeah. Should I be?"*

Quickly, he came back. *"I am. Have Wyatt trace her phone. I'm tied up, or I'd do it."*

"Will do. Text you what we learn." Sage's skin began to crawl. She knew from experience, Reggie would never ignore Shea's calls, especially when he was out on a mission. She ran to the living room, feeling blood drop from her face.

"Wyatt, something's wrong with Reggie. She's not taking calls from Shea and not answering his texts. He wants you to trace and locate her cellphone."

Wyatt laid the book in their son's lap and jumped to his feet. Whipping out his phone, he hit send. "Leo, I need you to locate Reggie Montgomery's cellphone immediately. Text me the location." Pause for a second. "Okay. Thanks."

Wyatt turned to Sage, worry creasing his forehead. "Leo is on duty. He's going to text me the second he finds her."

"You're not going this alone." It wasn't a question.

He smiled and pulled her into his arms. Her quivering limbs warmed by the heat of his immense body. "No worries. I'll take Leo as backup. Reggie will be okay. We all will."

"When did you last speak with her?" He scratched his head.

"Yesterday. I gave her the report from the cyber crime's investigation of the library computer used to make the carpet cleaning appointment for the missing girls house."

"I glanced through it in my inbox but didn't go into detail. Can you fill me in?"

Looking up into his poignant, blue, glistening eyes, she spoke tentatively. "Wyatt, I gave her a report last night on the IP address from the call. We found a local citizen and library patron named Marianne Knapp made the appointment. I gave Reggie Mrs. Knapp's address. Didn't she get someone to back her up today? Shea's out of town. Her team went back to their Louisville office. I assumed she'd ask you, Leo or Jaiden to accompany her. Oh crap, she's tracking that lead down alone."

"Son-of-a-bitch, that's exactly what she did."

Behind him, Ty slammed his crayon on the page. "Son-of-a-bitch."

She glanced around her husband with a stern look on her face. "Ty Gordon, you know better."

He shrugged. "Sorry, Mommy." He went back to his book.

"What the Knapp's address?" Wyatt met her gaze.

Wyatt's phone signaled a text. "*130 Plainfield Road, Sweetwater*." He flipped the screen toward Sage. "This it?"

Quivering started again and her face fell. "Yeah." Reggie was in danger.

Wyatt released her and texted Leo. "Meet me there NOW. I need backup. Call Jaiden. Tell her to join us." He ran to their bedroom and returned a moment later wearing his utility belt and checking his pistol.

"Wyatt, I promised not to follow the lead, but I did go to the courthouse to learn more about the Knapps. I did a title search and asked my team at Cyber to do a background check on them. Nothing much turned up. No criminal record. Not even a parking ticket for either of them.

Marianne married her husband Nathan when they were both twenty-one. They had one child. She died twenty-four years ago at six-year-old."

His face looked intense. "The child's name?"

"Magnolia Spring Knapp. She died of suffocation as result of tonsillectomy surgery.

"Magnolia!" His shoulders rose with a hearty inhale. "This is it. It's what we've been missing."

Her heart skipped a beat then tried to pound its way out of her chest as he rushed out the door slapping his hat on. "Lord, protect them."

Wyatt pulled out of his driveway. Jaiden's voice came over the call system. "Sheriff, I've located Reggie's vehicle."

"Where?" He wasn't known for wasting words.

"It's parked in a church lot across from the courthouse. It's unlocked. No sign of her."

"You check the trunk?" A surge of adrenaline filled his chest.

"Of course. Nothing, just her usual. Weapons, a go-bag with essentials and a change of clothing. Noting to indicate a problem. There's a fancy pair of high heels in the backseat."

"Fingerprint everything . . . well. Don't miss anything." He huffed and turned direction back toward Main Street.

Magnolia Blossoms

"Let Leo know we're swinging by there before moving on to the Knapp's address."

"You've got it, Boss." She disconnected.

Wyatt sped with lights on his truck until he reached the curvy road leading toward town. His skin prickled, and his hair crawled. Something was wrong, and Reggie was in danger. He knew better than to ignore his instincts. He'd develop a keen awareness over the years of policework. Since marrying his hippy-bred lovechild, Sage, he'd learned it could be honed and perfected. She was a huge fan of the human mystic powers God had bestowed.

They needed to use care. He didn't want to endanger her any more than she already was . . . Blare Moore either. A vision of the little girl's photo then one of Ty's cherub face flashed in his mind, sending a sharp pang from his heart to his gut.

He slowed down at the city limits and made his way through minor traffic, cars moving to the side to clear a path, to the courthouse. Jaiden and Leo's cruisers were parked beside Reggie's dark sedan.

"We've gone over this car and fingerprinted all handles, the trunk and hood, steering wheel, drink cozy, dashboard, radio and glove compartment door. Shea's and Reggie's prints are on file, as law enforcement. Theirs are the only ones we've discovered.

CHAPTER 21

Blare had gotten more comfortable with her and had crawled on top of her bed for a better view. "You were sleeping when they brought you in. Boy, you must've been tired. You still look sleepy."

Reggie gave her a bright smile. *Put it in words that aren't so scary . . . words a child can understand.* "I'm a little tired. I think they gave me something so I would rest. I'm okay now. How long was I asleep after they brought me here?"

Blare's shoulders rocked up and down. "Dunno. A while. I ate the lunch she brought me. She made my bed and helped me get dressed. Then she took the dishes away when they left. She always does that. If I don't eat it, I go hungry. She never leaves a tray here."

"That's fine. Was I asleep long after they left?"

"Just a little while. I was playing with my new stuffed animals."

"What did he do while they were here?"

Blare's mouth squeezed together. Her eyes narrowed. "He sat on the floor over there by the door and watched . . . after he got you sitting the way he wanted. I don't like it when he watches. He can say what he wants, but he's not my daddy." Her mouth went into a pout.

"No, he certainly is not. Are they treating you well? Has anyone hurt you? Are you getting enough to eat and drink?"

One shoulder tilted up. "Guess so. They bring breakfast, lunch and dinner. Sometimes, they bring a sandwich for lunch when they bring breakfast. There's a little cooler over here. They put drinks in it, so I can help myself. When they're not coming back for lunch, they put a sandwich in there too. I eat whenever I want it. Some of the food is yucky, but it's not all bad."

She looked healthy. It was a good sign. "I understand. I don't like somethings either. What did they bring you that was yucky?" She laughed trying to set the child at ease.

"Brissel sprouts. I don't like 'em. She made me take three bites and swallow them. It was disgusting." She made a sour face.

Reggie chuckled but didn't correct her. "I'm not fond of them either. You know what else I hate?"

"Unt'Uh." Her head shook.

"I hate corned beef. You ever had corned beef, Blare?"

Her nose curled a second and she smiled. "No. Mommy and Daddy had it on Patrick's Day. They asked if I wanted to try it. That nasty stuff stunk up the whole house when Mommy was cooking it. I didn't want to taste it. I'd never have got the taste off my tongue."

Reggie laughed appropriately, watching Blare become increasingly relaxed in Reggie's presence.

"These people are seriously mixed up." Blare frowned. "They're weirdos from outer space, I think. They keep trying to convince me Mommy and Daddy are dead, and they've adopted me. They said I'm their little girl now. I'm not a wacko, so I know that's not true. If it was, they'd have let me bring my toy, and I would be living in their

Magnolia Blossoms

house . . . with them. Not locked in this . . . room . . . alone." She teared up again.

"It's okay, Blare. You're not alone any longer. I'm here with you. We're in this together, and we're going to get you home to your real mommy and daddy." It was difficult staying in operative mode and not blubbering along with the child.

Damn it to hell. I need a weapon.

Her mind flashed on her phone. Had she pushed it soon enough and far enough they wouldn't find it. She stretched her neck. The thin chain of her 'special' anniversary gift moved as it settled against tender skin at the base of her neck.

Shea, where are you when I need you?

"Miss Reggie . . . these crazies want me to believe my name is now Maggie. He even called me Magnola."

"Magnolia?" Reggie asked.

"Yeah, ain't that a bush or something?"

"Actually, it's a tree and a flower from that tree. The couple who is holding you once had a daughter named Magnolia. I suppose they must've called her Maggie."

"Are they freaking nuts? They trying to make me think I'm her?"

"I suppose they are, Blare. I won't lie to you. I think they really miss her, and they want to love you so they're not too sad."

"Huh." Blare looked pensive.

"Blare, do you have anything among your toys or on your desk that is stiff and hard?" She desperately needed a tool to cut the zip ties behind her back. If they'd been in front, it would've been a breeze to snap them with a self-defense trick she'd learned.

Blare looked around. "No, I don't think so. I've got are some books, crayons and stuffed animals.

Reggie had figured it that way. These people had been keeping children in captivity for about twenty-four years. They knew a thing or two about keeping tools or items that could become makeshift weapons out of their hands. Soft items only, other than furniture. The bed and dresser were far from Reggie's reach. Even if she had a free hand, she couldn't pry anything off them that might be helpful.

"Have you ever screamed or cried out loudly, since you've been living here?"

"Yeah. That first day they stayed with me a long, long time."

"You know when I was sleeping, did you hear them say what they're planning to do about me?"

She pondered a moment. "I dunno. Maybe. She was sitting on the bed and looked at you real mean like. She said, "I don't like her being here." He was fussing with you in the corner and looked at her over his shoulder. "No worries," he said. "She won't be here long." "What are ya gonna do?" He gave her a mean look and kind a growled at her. "Same as the girls." I dunno what girls he was talking 'bout. I ain't seen nobody but them and you since they brung me here."

Just what Reggie expected. "Anything else?"

"Yeah, she told him he couldn't go back there."

"Did they mention where?" Marianne must've meant the farm where they'd found their previous victims.

"No, but he told her it weren't no never mind. He found another place." Blare's lower lip stuck out, and her chin wrinkled as she slumped on the bed.

"Did he say anything to describe this 'new' place?" *Please, let them have slipped up in front of the child.* They would assume Blare wouldn't understand.

"Only that he needed to scope—I think that's what he called it—scope it out once more." Blare's eyes teared up.

Magnolia Blossoms

"It's okay, Blare. You did really well. What you told me is super helpful. "

Yeah, right. Lie to the baby.

These assholes stole three children from their parents. Reggie would be damned if she was about to let them keep another one from her parents. They intended to kill Reggie anyway. She had nothing to lose.

I've got to find a way out of here. Something to use as a weapon.

"Those aren't the clothes your mommy dressed you in. Are they?" Twila had described in depth the clothing Blare had worn the day she was kidnapped.

"She made me change out of my shorts and shirt and put these goofy clothes on. She took my gymmers, and I ain't seen 'em since. I loved those shoes. They light up when I run fast. I'm stuck with these frilly, white socks. She brings me a new dress sometimes and takes the other one away to wash. I get clean jammies every day, too. I like sleep shorts, but she makes me wear a silly, ruffly gown that comes to my feet. I feel ridic-o-lus.'"

Reggie chuckled. "I get you. I like choosing my own wardrobe too. Frilly anything sucks. Don't you think?"

Blare spit out her first laugh since Reggie had arrived. "Yeah, you got that right. My daddy says that sometimes. 'That sucks wind,' he always says."

They laughed together.

"It sucks wind alright."

Sure, as shit does.

As Blare had said, no sound came from outside their small prison . . . until the door lock clicked a couple times. The thick, steel door creaked open.

A man came into view, pistol holstered to the belt of his frumpy jeans. He was probably early fifties. Thinning, grey hair topped an ordinary face. Nathan Knapp was the type of man one immediately forgot or never noticed in the first place. The delivery and repair person turned graveyard caretaker stood at tops five-foot-ten-inches tall. He was wiry and his frumpy cotton, button-down shirt hung on his slumped physique.

Marianne, on the other hand, was the type of female people wished they didn't know. She was a bitter crone with a broomstick up her rear, holding her rigid frame clean to the neck. The thin belt at her waist showed off a lumpy paunch, but other than that she had no shape. Broad shouldered, she stood at least three-inches taller than her mate. Her demeanor hadn't changed since Reggie had appeared on her doorstep.

Nathan shot Reggie a glare which dared her to speak. She craned her neck when his attention turned to Blare, trying to see what was outside the door. Nothing was visible from her position, not even through the hinged side crack. They left the door standing open, as they entered.

Blare hopped off the bed and straightened it then cowered in the desk chair. Her bright, keen eyes watched as though fearing their every move. Reggie's heart ached at the sight of the frightened child.

"Hi, Baby Girl. How's Daddy's Maggie doing today?" He ran a rough-looking palm over Blare's head. She flinched, but didn't pull back, though it was clear she wanted to.

His face softened as he stroked her cheek. Her eyes closed, as though blocking him out. Then he went to sit in a corner, where he could watch her and his wife, but keep an eye on Reggie at the same time. He shot her a nasty scowl as he adjusted his seat.

He had nothing to worry about . . . yet. Reggie wasn't about to try anything with herself bound like a Sunday dinner's rib roast.

Watch. Learn. Wait . . . for now. A weakness would show eventually. Sooner would work.

Magnolia Blossoms

Who knew how long they intended to keep her alive? Clearly, she was a problem they'd like solved quickly.

Marianne ignored Reggie, acting as though she wasn't in the room. A covered plate sat on the tray she carried. She sat it on the desktop. It held a single-serve milk carton, a cloth napkin wrapped around silverware, and a smaller dish with two plastic wrap covered cookies. Marianne paid complete attention to Blare.

"How's Mommy's Big Girl? Hungry? I made your favorite. Pot roast with mashed potatoes and gravy; those little, honeyed carrots you love and peas." She sat on the bedside watching Blare at the desk. "Eat your meat and veggies, and you can have the cookies."

"I hate peas." Blare opened the napkin and laid it across her lap.

Who had trained the little girl to do that? Her mother or Marianne?

Wouldn't want to piss of Mrs. Wackadoodle.

"Now, Maggie, you know you love them. Eat up, Sweetie. Daddy and Mommy have work to do."

Yeah, covering up loose trails from abducting a Federal Agent. You dumb son-of-a-bitches have no clue what you've done. They were about to face the full force of the law . . . soon as Reggie got out of this dungeon.

Were they below ground? That would make locating them more difficult.

Resolved and relieved, they hadn't brought her a meal, Reggie studied the loving family's interactions. He was clearly the quiet one. She was the driving force of their relationship. Which one was the brains of this operation—the one who had concocted this little plan—the one who had done the dirty work, killed three lovely children? Children they'd professed to love, whom they'd cared for over a six-year period.

Blare isn't wrong about you assholes.

Magnolia Blossoms

CHAPTER 21

Wyatt had phoned the judge from the lot and explained the situation. Leo ran inside the courthouse to his chambers to get the search warrant. While they waited, Wyatt rang Shea.

He picked up immediately. "Wyatt, tell me you found Reggie."

"Man, I'd love to. We've located her car and have a good lead as to what she might've been investigating today. Leo pinged her phone to the address in question, so we know she's there. At least, we think so. I wanted to let you know the situation before we serve the warrant."

"I'm delivering the judge in an hour to his residence. This mission is over. I should be back in Sweetwater in about three hours."

"We don't have time to wait."

"No, please move forward. Wyatt, bring my woman home safely."

"Will do. I'll ring you after we finish." They clicked off.

Leo returned. The three of them suited up in Kevlar vests. Leo with paperwork in hand. He stuck it in his back pocket. Jaiden and Leo placed their heavy weaponry in Wyatt's locked truck compartment. The three of them checked handguns and backup firearms to ensure they were ready. Jaiden ran a palm over her long knife and slid into Wyatt's passenger seat. Leo climbed into the rear seat.

Magnolia Blossoms

Dusk was setting in. Nightfall would soon take over. Doom and gloom might be prevalent in the darkness, but in the cap of Wyatt's truck three well-honed law enforcement professionals were mentally doing what they had to do to get into battle mode.

He sped up as they exited city limits. The winding road out of town took them to Paradise Lane. A right turn would bring them toward Wyatt's and Sage's home, toward her organic farm and toward Mane Lane Farm, Levi Madison's horse racing farm. Instead, Wyatt took a quick left turn.

Going well past speed limit, they zipped along the highway. Little traffic that time on a weekday, allowed them to forego the siren. Soon they turned onto a short, dead-end lane ending at the Knapp residence.

The non-descript, brick ranch sat on a spacious, fenced lot of about an acre-and-a-half. Enough dusky light remained in the day, he could make out a couple of aged magnolia trees in the pristinely cut back lawn.

Wyatt's heart did a double-tap, and he exited the truck. "No vehicles visible. No garage, only a driveway."

Leo stepped out and flipped the cargo section open. "Records show they own a 2010 Chevrolet sedan."

"Suit up." Wyatt opened the cargo section from his side and pulled out his Colt M4 carbine.

Jaiden joined Leo and selected her Remington 700 sniper rifle and flipped the band around her shoulder. Leo picked up his SIG Sauer P226 9 mm. They all had handguns at their waists and backups at their ankles.

Of course, Jaiden carried her pig sticker. "Looks like no one's home."

Wyatt gave her a wary grin. "Probably want it to look that way. Be on your toes."

With a nod from his deputies, Leo and Wyatt approached the door. Jaiden ran around back in case someone tried to light out that way. He pushed the button.

A melodious chime echoed inside. After a few seconds with no answer, he rang the bell again. Again, no answer came. He knocked loudly. "Mr. and Mrs. Knapp, this is Sheriff Gordon. Open up." He pounded the door once again.

Leo stepped to the corner of the house, looked toward the rear. Jaiden's Texas-Kentucky twang informed him, "No movement or sound back here. I don't think they're home."

Wyatt moved aside. "Can you open it?"

Leo stepped to the door, pulled out a toolkit and fumbled with the lock. Seconds later a click and Leo opened the door. "Easy, peasy. These folks must feel pretty secure in their secret to have such flimsy locks."

Wyatt frowned. "Doesn't make me feel so secure. Means they might not keep anything incriminating here."

"Guess we'll find out." Leo stepped in; gun drawn. "Sheriff's office. We're coming in." He carefully strolled through the house, checking each room before entering. In the kitchen, he unlocked the back door to let Jaiden in.

"No sign of them or any vehicles out back."

The three donned vinyl gloves and searched the rooms of the two-bedroom cottage. There were two toothbrushes in the bath and nothing that indicated the presence of a child. The bed was made with a quilted spread and shams. No clothing was present outside of the closet, where everything hung neatly. Nathans clothing on one side and Marianne's on the other.

A glance in the medicine cabinet showed nothing unusual. No chemicals to drug or murder with. No syringes. Nothing to treat a child.

Jaiden reported nothing of suspect in cabinets or drawers. There was no pantry. The table held only a plate of napkins, salt and pepper shaker. The gleaming oven was empty and cold. No poisons, drugs or significant finds under the spotless sink. Contents of the refrigerator provided no clue.

"Boss, there's no basement door inside," Leo reported from the bedroom.

"No entrance to a cellar or basement outside either," Jaiden assured them.

The living room was exceedingly tidy. Magazines were stowed in chair-side tables. Pristine doilies had been starched to ruffle and dared a spot of dust to land on them.

"Leo, call the CSI Team. I want them to go over this joint with a microscope. If there's a blade of Reggie's or Blare's hair inside this house or on this half-acre lot, I want it found." Wyatt recognized his voice had turned to a bellow. He shrugged it off. His team understood.

A child's life was at stake. Everyone was on edge. Reggie wasn't just a co-worker. She'd been in his life since kindergarten, and she was their friends, too.

"Jaiden, call the FBI office. Let them know Reggie's missing. Any luck, we'll find her before they get here from Louisville. God willing."

The mantle held a photograph of the couple on their long-ago wedding date. Another photo showed the couple at a younger age with their toddler daughter, Magnolia.

A shiver sizzled down Wyatt's spine.

Wyatt continued looking around, then he pulled out his phone and rang a number. A quiet hum sounded . . . a vibration. Keenly listening he followed the buzz. He flipped the cushion up from the seat revealing a phone—Reggie's phone. Vibrations stopped. Wyatt hit 'send' again, and the cellphone pulsated in his hand. He clicked 'stop,' and it ceased.

"Hot damn, that gal is cagy. She'd been aware something was up, and she was in danger, and she'd had the presence of mind to stuff her cell between the seat and cushion. It was a miracle the Knapps hadn't found it, given how many calls Reggie had received from those trying to contact her. He should've known she'd do what she could to leave a trail. Reggie was a trained professional. Even the best can be bushwhacked. Reggie missing proved that.

He had to find her. Sage would never forgive him if he failed. Reggie was the sister Sage never had.

Hell. He'd never forgive himself.

Shea? Shea would have no mercy. He would blame himself . . . and Wyatt.

Yep, and I'd deserve it. I should've partnered with her while Shea was out of town.

"How are we going to play this, Sheriff?" Leo eyed him, lips taunt and Jaiden by his side.

"Suits will be here in about three hours. They're not in Louisville. They're assisting on another case in Cincinnati, breaking free of it soon and coming straight here."

"Shea should be here soon. Here's what we're doing."

He informed Leo to move the cruiser down the lane and to the church lot around a bend. Then he'd return on foot. They shut the doors and waited.

Magnolia Blossoms

181

CHAPTER 22

The door slammed shut, and a couple clicks later they were locked in again. No sound came, though Reggie strained to hear, as they left. No climbing or descending of steps. No doors opening and closing past their prison room. No vehicles coming to life. Nothing.

Reggie drove disappointment away. It wasn't time. She needed a cool head to think.

"You okay, Blare?"

The girl turned from facing the desk against the far wall. "Uh huh. Are you, Miss Reggie?"

"I'm good. You know what?" She smiled, trying to lighten the mood.

"What?" Blare's sad expression turned curious. She clutched her stuffed bunny.

"You and I are partners in this. I'm sure your parents taught you to show respect by calling grown ups Miss, but this is a special situation between us. I believe they'd agree. It's okay for you to call me Reggie—just Reggie. You okay with that?"

Her head nodded, and beginnings of a smile showed on her face. "Uh huh."

"Good, then partner, I need your help."

"I can't do nothing. I'm tied to this bed," Blare reminded her.

"I know, but there is something you can do. Why don't you climb on the bed and get as close to this side as you can without falling? I don't want you to hurt your ankle, so hold onto the chain as you do, to stretch it straight as far as you can. Can you do that?"

"Guess so." She stood, laid her bunny on the desk, and bent to secure her confines.

Reggie forced herself to topple onto her side. She landed hard on what felt like carpeting covered concrete.

A slab room or basement?

She scooted awkwardly and difficultly toward the bed, arms and shoulders aching. She wobbled and flopped like a catfish out of water, consistently banging her head. Eventually, she managed to get near the bedside nearest to her.

Exhausted from her efforts, she laid on her side staring up at bright lighting from the aged, drop ceiling. It was a pattern made three decades before and had been painted at least once. There wasn't a dust bunny one beneath the pretty, little girl's bed.

That sent adrenaline surging through her veins. She shifted her weight until she could prop up to a sideways slump. Using her tied hands to push herself the reminder of the way, she groaned and flipped upward to a sit atop her bent legs and bound feet. With a hearty inhale, she smiled. Thank goodness for her diligent, extreme workouts and sparring sessions with Shea. Her tight abdomen and strong back muscles were coming in handy. Muscled or not, her body ached from skin to bone in every place possible, and strain on her shoulders was excruciating.

"Hey, girl. How ya doing?" She grinned.

Blare giggled into her hands. "You looked funny, rolling around on the floor."

"Well, I am funny." She chuckled, sticking her tongue out, arching her brows and wiggling her face into a comical expression. "Some folks say I'm a clown. You aren't afraid of clowns. Are you, Blare?" Shea wasn't afraid of much, but he hated clowns. She never missed an opportunity to poke fun at him about it.

"Heck no. I saw one at the county fair. He pulled about a million hankies out of his nose." Blare tittered.

"Well, once we get out of here, we'll have tons of time to clown around. You and I are going to become great pals." Hopefully, this wasn't another lie to her little friend. "Right now, I need you do to something I can't with my hands tied behind me."

"I can't reach your hands to untie them." Blare glowered.

"I know, Sweetheart. But you can lean over the edge of the bed and, if I lean forward, you can reach my neck. Think you can do that?"

Tiny shoulders rocked up and down. Clearly, Blare wasn't sure she could stretch far enough.

"It's okay. You can do it. I'm going to lean forward, and you're going to grab the bangle at my neck—the one on the chain. See it?" She flipped her curls with a toss of the head, to ensure her hair didn't block Blare's view of the necklace.

"That sparkly thing? It's bootiful."

"Thank you. Yes. It is, and that's it. Now, when you get it in your hand, you're going to feel around the back. There's a lever there. It's hidden at the top, where the chain runs through it. It's very tiny and not easy to see. Okay, ready?"

Blare nodded. She laid down on her belly and moved far as she could without tumbling off the bed. Reggie straightened up on her knees then bent as far as she could.

Blare's tiny hand wrapped around the pendant. "It's smooth back there."

"Yes, now move your finger to where the chain runs through the bangle." The miniature hand shifted at her neck. "Feel it"

"Uh huh."

"Great. Use your fingernail. Move it. It will only shift one way. If it doesn't budge, try another direction."

"Got it. That was easy. Boy, this does sparkle." Blare's adorable blue eyes opened wide eyeing the piece.

She smiled and kissed the tiny hand as Blare released her necklace. The diamond and platinum piece landed between Reggie collar bone.

"Thank you, Blare. That was perfect. You can move back further on the bed. I don't want you to fall."

The poor baby was uncomfortable enough with that metal, ankle cuff. She'd gotten a fair look at it as the child had hauled it to the edge of the bed. At least it wasn't a stun cuff.

"You want some water? I've got some in that little frigidator." She glanced over her shoulder. "They didn't bring you no dinner." Blare asked, propped on her knees like how Reggie sat.

"I'd love some. Do you have enough? I don't want you to go thirsty."

"There are four in there. I counted 'em. I can count to fifty. Want to hear?"

"Maybe later, when I get settled." Reggie smiled at the child-like switch from subject to subject.

"I won't drink that much before tomorrow." Blare hopped down and returned soon with a plastic bottle. She twisted the bottle with apparent force. "I'm a big girl now. I can open bottles myself. Some bottle." She grinned, and her eyes sparkled.

"Yes, you are. You're a very smart, capable girl." Reggie leaned forward and allowed the child to pour water into her gaping mouth.

Blare fed her the liquid slowly and carefully, as though she dared not spill any. As Reggie swallowed, she waited.

"Thank you, Blare. That was thoughtful of you. I feel much better now. That's enough." She sure as hell didn't want to give Knapp satisfaction of peeing herself.

"Okay." Blare cheerfully capped the top and hopped off the bed. She returned to the bed, soon as the bottle was stored, bringing her bunny along.

"I'm going to lay here and rest for a minute." She plopped on the hard floor on her side. Her back, shoulders and limbs ached.

"I'm really sleepy." Blare's bed creaked from her movement. From her line of sight, Reggie noted the mattress was held up by a bed board instead of a box spring or simple spring support. A spring might be useful. No help there.

"Why don't you lie down and take a rest. I'll wake you when it's time to go." Assuming she could fight her way out of her constraints and, by some miracle, get them out the locked door.

"I'd better put my jammies on first. She gets really mad if I fall asleep in my clothing."

"Good idea. You'll be more comfortable that way."

Sounds of the child slipping out of her garments and into the long nightgown came above where Reggie rested, trying to regain her strength. Before long, a soft purr came from the bed.

Reggie scooted and wriggled until she lay with her backside to the door. She did the hop-wiggle-hop maneuver again, bringing her to her knees. Leaning a shoulder against cold steel of the door, she waggled until her arm wrapped over the doorknob. Putting all her weight on the arm braced against the knob, she forced her face downward toward the floor. This caused her arm to slide along the knob until it met the binding around her wrist. At the same time, her knees were lifted off the floor and rose alone the metal door. She dangled face down by her wrist.

Ignoring slicing of agonizing flesh at her wrists, she used her hands to scoot the zip tie binding her hands past the knob, moving her weight onto supported of the strip connecting her hands to her feet. The slim plastic strip stretched ever so slightly as she moved, but not enough. She jerked her body against it several times, and it gave way more, bit-by-bit. So did the skin on her wrists and ankles. With a deep, cleansing breath she yanked head and feet downward with all her might.

Snap.

Reggie tumbled face first to the floor. She laid there a few seconds, regaining her breath that had been knocked out of her chest on impact with concrete.

Her hands remained tied behind her, and her feet were still bound, but she could stretch out on the solid surface. Muscles relaxed some with hands freed from being attached to her feet. Blood surged through deprived limbs. Intense needle pricks of pain pulsed in her shoulders, arms and legs as fresh blood flooded the regions. She clenched and unclenched fists and wriggled ankles and toes to hurry the process along. Her neck ached from struggle, and she rolled her head to relieve tension. Her arms felt as though they'd been wrenched from their sockets. She rolled her shoulders a few times.

She wasn't free by any means, but she was one step closer to freedom.

CHAPTER 23

Jaiden stood guard in the Knapp's kitchen, in case Nathan and Marianne entered that way. Leo was hidden in the tree line outside, to prevent escape. Wyatt sat in the living room facing the front door. It wasn't long before car engine droned from the lane, and tires chewed the gravel drive.

Wyatt's hand went to the automatic laying beside his hand on the arm of the chair. He stood, gripped it and released the safety sure his people were doing the same.

The motor went silent. Steps crunched the rock walk and went silent as the walker took the three steps. The lock clicked, and the door swung open.

A tall, stiff-moving female stood in the doorway. Her pale face blanched whiter, and her eyes flew wide. Her lips pressed and repressed, as though she fought the urge to let it flop open. "What in the blazes are you doing here, Sheriff Gordon." It was a reproach, like that of a grade-school nun who had caught a pupil chewing gum in class.

Wyatt snickered. "I believe you know what I'm doing here. Are you alone?" He leaned to glance around her.

Outside Leo waved a hand indicating she was not accompanied. With a glace at the lane, to see if another vehicle followed, Leo walked to her car. Leo knew his role. He would look inside it, pop the trunk and make sure neither kidnapped victim was stowed there.

"Yes, not that it's any of your business; and I have no clue, why you've taken the liberty to enter my home without permission." She took a couple steps toward him.

Wyatt flipped the search warrant out. "I have the right to search these premises, your vehicles and any other properties owned or leased by you and your husband. Where is Nathan?"

She took the paper, which enunciated a quiver in her hand. "I have no idea where he is. I wouldn't tell you if I did."

"I expected as much." He pointed to a chair. "Where are they, Marianne? We know you have them?" He sat on the coffee table, leaning toward her, a harsh expression on his face.

"I told you." She pursed her lips up, glowering at the ceiling then back at him. "I don't know where Nathan is. I have no idea when he will return, but I expect him to be late."

"I see. Well then, you're coming with us." He stood, taking a reluctant hand from her. "Mrs. Marianne Knapp." He read her rights, in case and assuming he'd be arresting her later that night. "I need you to come with me to the Precinct to answer some questions. You are a person-of-interest."

"Sheriff, surely you jest. I'm an upstanding citizen. I have 'no interest' in being involved in any sort of criminal investigation."

He ushered her out the door. "Mrs. Knapp, you're about to learn. I have no sense of humor and never joke about anything to do with the law." He helped her easily into the back seat of the cruiser Leo had just parked in front of the house. Jaiden had joined them to stand by the car.

Leo stepped out. "What's the play her, Sheriff?"

"Leo, stay here. Call Francis and Martin to come help you as backup. Wait for the Mr. to return. I'll keep you informed, should we get him before he returns here. Jaiden and I will take Mrs. Knapp to the station to be interrogated. We need to pry the location or locations where they're holding Reggie and Blare, out of her pasty-faced mouth. I'll drive. Jaiden, text Shea to meet us there when he arrives."

The Precinct was nearly empty. A couple deputies were out on patrol, and others were off for the night. Reggie deposited their guest in an interrogation room. Wyatt turned the heat up in that room and went to the room adjoining it to keep an eye on the strange woman. "Go check and see if the Knapps have any other properties."

"You've got it, Sheriff." On duty his staff was diligent about addressing him with his title, though Jaiden and Leo were dear personal friends. Jaiden disappeared into the bullpen.

Marianne sat stiffly in the uncomfortable chair, wrists chained to the stainless-steel table, she clasped hands together. Her shoulders remained back, and she focused on a corner with a security camera mounted at the ceiling.

Shea returns. They're interrogating Marianne. He's not been able to get a signal on the tracking device on her necklace tracker. Sweat began to glisten her forehead and pale, lined cheeks. Her lips wrinkled looking forced into a closed circle. She had to be uneasy but did not show it.

Shea peeked his head into the room. "Jaiden said you'd be in here. How long has that woman been sitting there?" He head-nodded toward the woman Wyatt had been observing through the one-way window, and he shook the hand Wyatt offered.

"Half an hour. She's about ready. I've been giving Jaiden time to research something for me." It wasn't the sole reason for delaying interrogation. Wyatt liked his them confused, nervous and uncomfortable when he probed them. "We located Reggie's phone at the Knapp residence. This is Marianne Knapp. Her husband, Nathan, is AOL. So far, Marianne has been unhelpful. She's about ready. Want to observe?"

"Yeah, make her talk, Wyatt."

"It's my goal." He slapped Shea's back and exited the room into the hallway. A second later, he entered the sweltering room. Marianne glanced up, then began to stare at her hands. The knuckles were white, as she gripped them tightly. "Watch from here." Wyatt exited the viewing room.

Seconds later Marianne Knapp sat stiffly in the interrogation room. Her wrists were attached to metal cuffs attached to the steel table in front of her. Sweat beaded across her forehead and cheeks. Dampness darkened fabric underneath her shoulders of her prim, floral, housedress. Her facial muscles appeared to be straining to maintain an air of distain. Her head turned, and she glared at Wyatt as he walked in then stared at the far end of the table.

Wyatt's lanky frame ambled toward the table, and he folded it into the chair across from her. He sat two bottles of water on the table. Opening one, he took a long sip. "Ah."

Her gaze refused to meet his, as she continued to avoid him. Tiny wrinkles formed around her pinched lips.

"Mrs. Knapp, we know you and your husband, Nathan, kidnapped FBI Special Agent Reggie Montgomery and have evidence you and Mr. Knapp kidnapped Blare Moore. We have reason to believe you have kept Blare Moore alive. For your sake, I hope you've done the same for

Magnolia Blossoms

Agent Montgomery. It would be to your advantage to cooperate and help us locate your husband, Agent Montgomery and Miss Moore."

"This is ridiculous. You people are insane. I'm guilty of nothing. Release me now, and you can avoid a nasty lawsuit." Her harsh tone came in a muffled voice.

Wyatt snickered, as he eased back in his chair, drawing an elbow to rest on the chair back. "I'm afraid we will not be releasing you. You'd best save your money for a decent defense lawyer. Now, where has your husband gone off to, and where are you holding Blare Moore?"

"I have no idea where Nathan has gone."

"We gave an APB out on him. My fellow law enforcement officers know he's a child murderer and that he has at least kidnapped one of their own. We take these two heinous crimes extremely seriously. Nathan will be caught. If you want him apprehended alive, I'd suggest you tell us what you know."

She shot him a stare that was meant to burn a hold though his soul. "Nathan didn't tell me where he was going."

At least she was looking at him now. "Okay, what did he tell you?" Wyatt took another sip of his water.

Marianne's eyes grazed across the unopened bottle. Condensation had formed on it in the heated room, and it trickle down the plastic to puddle around the container on the metal surface. She rubbed her lips together, and her jaw moved in a swallowing motion, though her lips never opened.

"Nathan went hunting." She gruffly pushed words out.

"Well, let's see," Wyatt drawled. "Deer season is the only one in now. Gun season ended last weekend. Does he hunt with a bow or a crossbow?" Primitive weapons were the only legal means of hunting deer at the time of year. "I wasn't aware Nathan was a hunter. Did he go alone?"

Her stiff shoulders rocked up and down. "I have no idea."

"When did you last see him?"

"When he got off work."

"When do you expect him home?"

Without looking at Wyatt she shook her head slowly. "Sheriff, I have no idea. Nathan often stays out all night when hunting."

Wyatt tilted his head, acting as though he believed her. "Overnight you say. So, does he have a hunting cabin somewhere? Does he sleep in a tent? Hunting deer after dark is illegal, you know."

He wasn't going to get anywhere on this line of questioning. When she failed to answer, Wyatt took a long draw on his bottle. "So, where are you keeping Blare Moore, and is Agent Montgomery with her?"

Her eyes met his, and pure evil stared back at him. "I don't know anyone named Blare Moore."

"Alright. How about Agent Montgomery? Where is she?" He sat his bottle down and sat a bit straighter.

"How would I know?"

"Well, we know she visited you today. We found her phone lodged in your sofa."

She acted almost congenial, easing facial muscles a bit. "How would I know where she went when she left?"

"You were the last person to see her. We found her vehicle a couple miles from your home. It's obvious she didn't drive it there and leave it."

Her head rocked a tiny measure and she glared into his eyes. "And how in the world can you know that?"

"Whomever drove her car was taller and had adjusted the seat to reach the pedals. That person made the mistake of not moving the seat back up. We know; Agent Montgomery can only reach them by having the seat pulled all the way forward."

Magnolia Blossoms

She snorted and looked away.

"Are you that person, Mrs. Knapp? Did you move Agent Montgomery's automobile, so it wouldn't be found at your home? We believe she put her phone in your couch on purpose, so we could find her there."

"As you know, Sheriff, that flashy little twerp of a woman is not at my home." Surprisingly, spit didn't spew from her lips as she spoke.

A buzz came on his phone, a text from Jaiden. Wyatt stood, leaving the water sitting and walked toward the door. "Excuse me a second, Mrs. Knapp." He closed the door behind him.

In the hallway, Jaiden and Shea waited. "Sheriff, Reggie's phone battery was nearly exhausted when we found it. I recharged the battery. She left it on Record. Listen to this."

Jaiden clicked the button and Reggie's voice came from the gadget. "Yes, well, we have proof you made that appointment."

Shea let out a moan. Wyatt leaned closer to the phone to hear now muffled sounds. A moan, then Reggie went quiet. Other voices took over—voices of Nathan and Marianne arguing. They listened to the noise until a door slammed and it went quiet.

Jaiden turned it off. "It goes on with nothing for a long time. Then sounds of us breaking in, searching and then arresting Mrs. Knapp come on."

Wyatt nodded and took the phone. "Good work, Jaiden." She turned toward the bullpen. Shea went back into the viewing area, and Wyatt carried the phone into the interrogation room.

Sitting, he laid the phone on the tabletop. "Do you know what this is?"

Marianne shrugged. "I suppose you're going to tell me."

"How about I show you." He clicked the recording device on, and Marianne's bluster lost much of its air.

"Thank goodness you came home early." She stared at the device as her voice came from it. The discussion between her and Nathan went on after Reggie's moan. It was a clear admission between them that he would take her vehicle and ditch it. She drove their car with an unconscious Reggie in the trunk and picked him up at the church where he parked Reggie's vehicle. They agreed to taker Reggie to '*Maggie's*' room temporarily, until he could figure out how to '*dispose*' of her.

"You've got to get rid of her quick. I don't want her there with Maggie, no longer than she has to be."

"Yeah, well, I need one more scouting trip, to make sure no one will find her body at the place I found."

She'd grumbled a bit and some grunting and groaning accompanied what sounded like them carrying Reggie out.

Wyatt flipped the phone off. "Who is Maggie?"

Marianne gave him a hateful stare. "My daughter."

Wyatt wasn't surprised. "I see. Yes, I'm aware you and Nathan had a daughter. My condolences. I understand your daughter died twenty-four-years ago."

She glowered at a ceiling corner. Lips pressed together.

"Marianne, there's terrible grief when losing a child. I sympathize with your loss. Maggie was about six, according to her death certificate. That's the same age as Blare Moore. Did you take Blare to replace your dead daughter, Maggie?"

"Sheriff, you have no idea what you're talking about."

His phone buzzed. He read a text from the forensic scientist. "Unfortunately for you, I do." He showed her his phone, though not the message. "We have identified evidence from your trunk that Agent Montgomery was in there." He gave that a second to set in. "We also have matched scrapes of fabric and lace in your sewing basket with that worn by another of your victims, the young teenaged girl discovered on a farm outside of town. It appears you made that child's dress and sewed lace around her stockings . . . before you murdered her."

Her head snapped to stare him in the eyes. "I didn't murder nobody."

"So, Nathan did the deed? Did he also kill the other two girls we unearthed from the same property? They were wearing similar clothing. Dressed the same. Had the same hair style. Were they also replacements for Maggie?"

She sniffed an inhale and stared again at the ceiling.

"You and Nathan kidnapped these girls, kept them in captivity from their families until they approached puberty, then discarded them like yesterday's trash when they no longer reminded you of your little Maggie." These despicable people made Wyatt nauseous.

She blinked moisture forming in her bitter eyes, continuing to gaze at the ceiling corner.

"Marianne, did it ever occur to you that you were causing the same pain of loss you and Nathan had for the parents of the girls you abducted? You've put four sets of parents in agony for years. We'll return remains of the girls you and Nathan cold-bloodedly murdered, to their loved ones. At least, they have closure now. You stole lives of those young girls. You stole the love of their parents and family."

Her eyes batted. A stream of tears streamed from one eye down her ridged, placid cheek.

"You cared for these girls. I see it in your face. It was clear from the way you buried them. You loved them."

Another batt of her eyes, and the tears stopped.

"You love little Maggie—the one you have locked away somewhere."

Her head nodded without a change of expression or other movement.

"Help us find her. . . before Nathan kills her too." She didn't give a rat's ass about Reggie. She did care about Blare though, or *Maggie*. He had to work on that edge.

Her head jerked almost imperceptibly.

"Marianne, help us save Maggie. Help us find Nathan. If we don't locate Nathan before he discovers you've been arrested, he'll kill Maggie. Either that, or he'll try to escape and leave her to die. She'll die a painful death. Do you understand how agonizing it is to starve to death? To go without water. Starvation causes edema, bodily fluid inflammation. This will be excruciatingly painful for Maggie. Maggie will suffer an enlarged, fatty liver resulting in a distended belly." He held hands in front of his stomach, showing what he meant.

She glanced at his gesture then returned eyes to a distance.

"Maggie will suffer from muscle loss, atrophy and finally organ failure. She'll develop skin lesions and with a disrupted immune system due to starvation, they'll get infected. Maggie's mouth will go dry, caked and thickly coated. Maggie's lips will become parched and crack painfully. Maggie's tongue will swell and crack. Maggie's eyes will recede back into their orbits. Her cheeks will hollow. Her nose lining will crack. Maggie's nose will bleed. Skin will hang loosely, dry out and become scaly. Maggie's bladder will burn as her urine thickens and becomes highly concentrated. Maggie's stomach will dry out, causing dry heaves and vomiting. She'll experience extremely high temperatures. Brain cells will dry out causing Maggie to experience convulsions."

Marianne's already pale face turned a light, sea foam green. "Maggie's respiratory tract will dry out and secretions will plug her lungs so she can't breathe. Her main organs—heart, lungs, brain—will give out. The brain requires chemical signals, electrolyte balance, to function properly. As the brain dries, electrolytes deteriorate. The brain fails to operate. Maggie will become lethargic, unable to move. Maggie will suffer from an excruciating heart attack, caused by rotting from the inside out, as her organs dry up."

A sniff, but nothing else came from the bizarre woman.

"You may not have killed the previous 'Maggie's' by your own hands, but you are responsible just the same. If you don't help us find Nathan, you're causing Maggie to die an agonizing death. Is that what you want?"

Her head jerked to look at him with pure hatred. "You bastard, what kind of monster do you think I am? Nathan promised me those girls went peacefully in their sleep, that they didn't feel any pain."

Right, and she believed that?

"They were smothered to death in their sleep. Maggie, however, may not go that way. If Nathan doesn't return to care for her, she's going to die a miserable, painful death. That will be your doing, Marianne. You'll have to live with visions of Maggie's excruciating demise in your mind . . . as long as the justice system allows you to live."

She inhaled so hard it sounded like she was sucking something solid through her stern nostrils.

His phone buzzed. Jaiden had texted. *I KNOW WHERE THEY'RE AT.* Wyatt stood and pocketed his phone. "Too late, you've had time to help. The court will know you sentenced Blare Moore and FBI Agent Reggie Montgomery to death.

As Wyatt walked toward the door, her face swung toward him. "I didn't."

"I'll send an officer to take you to your cell and give you some water." He disappeared out the door.

CHAPTER 24

Reggie lay face down on the carpeted concrete floor. Her chin burned from slamming against the non-padded surface as she'd fallen. Her hands were still bound with a cord behind her back, as where her feet; but she was grateful to be able to stretch out. Damned Nathan Knapp had trust her up like a goose on Sunday morning. Son-of-a-bitch intended to kill and bury her the way he'd done the three victims they'd uncovered. It wasn't happening if Reggie had anything to do with it. Her demise would seal poor Blare Moore's fate. She wasn't having that on her eternal conscious.

She scootched and squirmed until she made it to the bedside. The child was softly purring in her sleep. Reggie hated to interrupt the angel's slumber, but better her do it than Nathan Knapp. His disposal farm had been discovered. He was, undoubtedly, looking over a fresh place to bury his captives. If Reggie couldn't get free, Blare was likely going to witness her death, which would have a more devastating effect on the child than Reggie's waking her.

"Blare." Reggie put on the voice she used when reporting news to loved ones, the soft, comforting one she'd practiced and used over her many years working for the FBI. "Blare, honey, wake up. I need your help."

The girl sat up in bed rubbing her eyes with tiny fists. "Mommy?" She blinked a few times.

Reggie smiled. "No, Sweetie. It's me, Reggie."

Tears started to swell in Blare's eyes. "Is it morning, Reggie? Time to go home to Mommy and Daddy?"

"Not morning, Blare. I need your help. We're partners in this. So, partner, can you come down here and help me with something?

"Guess so." Blare pushed the blankets back and slid to the floor.

Reggie's backside faced her, as she sat on the carpet. "See this strip of plastic I'm holding in my hand?" It was the broken one that had secured her hands to her feet.

"Yeah."

"Good. Take it." Blare took the piece. "Now, look between my hands at the section where the band goes through a little box like thing. It runs through a little tunnel."

Blare inspected Reggie's bound hands. "Yeah, I see it."

"Good. You're doing well, Blare. Now take the piece you're holding and slip it into that little tunnel, with the other piece."

Blare's warm, soft hands fumbled with the contraption for a few minutes then she sat back on her heels. "It won't go in." Her voice was heavy with defeat.

"That's okay, Blare. How about you turn the piece over and try it that way?" It would only fit one way. Blare had eliminated one, so it should fit the opposite direction.

Again, the softness of Blare's hands made Reggie's chest swell with longing. Longing to save this little girl. Longing to give birth to one of her own. A longing that had troubled her since she'd fallen for Shea, and her maternal instinct had forced her to admit time was running out. She was nearing forty. Her ability to bear a child was passing quickly. Too quickly. Time was also running out for her to save Blare. Too quickly.

Blare plopped back on her heels with a grin on her adorable face. "It went in."

Reggie tugged her hand apart. The zip tie gave way, sliding unhinged by the channel with the strip Blare had inserted forcing the teeth down. She wrung her hands together. "You did it, Blare." Reggie held a hand up.

Blare slapped Reggie's palm with a glow in her eyes. "Your hands are free, but you're bleeding."

Reggie inspected her injured wrists. Flesh had been grated bare, and parts had begun to clot. "It's not so bad." She smiled at the little girl and stood. "Can I use a couple of your fluffy hair ties?" She picked up two fabric-covered ones from the desk dresser.

"Sure/" Blare shrugged. "They're not mine anyway. Nothing here is mine. That woman keeps trying to convince me they are and that I'm their little girl. They call me Maggie. I don't care what they say. My name is Blare."

"Darned right it is, Blare." Reggie put the ties around her wrists, to cover the damage, more so it wouldn't upset Blare than to protect her wounds. They would heal and not leave long-lasting scars.

Reggie picked up the strip Blare had used to release her hands and fed the end of it into the channel of the ties securing her feet together. Pulling the one around her ankles apart, the band slipped easily, loosening its hold.

She pushed it off her feet, wriggled them a few seconds and inspected the damage. Not as bad as her wrists, but tender flesh just the same. She stood and shook her slacks down to cover the sight. No sense in worrying the child more than she already was.

"Blare, sit back on your bed. I'm going to break that dresser and mirror. I don't want stray pieces cutting you."

"Okay." She climbed on the bed and sat beside the pillow.

Reggie knelt and inspected the desk. She shoved the few items atop it onto the floor and lifted one side by a leg. With a hearty jerk, she loosened glue helping hold it together. With a sturdy twist, she gritted her teeth and yanked as hard as she could. The bolt holding the leg to the top gave way and turned. She continued spiraling it until it released. She studied the end. A bolt end about two inches long stuck out of the top of the leg. It would make a decent weapon.

She stood and held the leg over her shoulder like a bat. Swinging it like she intended to hit a ball into the outfield, she forced the end of it against the mirror. The glass shattered. A few chips flew across the floor where the table had sat, but none as far as where Blare sat on the bed. Most broken pieces stayed attached at one end to the round mirror's frame.

"Perfect." She laid the leg down and gazed around. "Blare, do you care about that bunny you were hugging before you went to sleep?"

Blare looked at the pile of stuffed animals in the corner and shrugged. "Not really. None of those things are mine. I just needed something to cuddle. You know. When I was scared."

"I totally understand. When I'm frightened, a hug helps me too." She bent and picked up the toy rabbit. "Since you don't mind, I'm going to use this bunny." Sitting on the bedside, she yanked the ears hard. Stitching began to give way. She stuck her finger inside the seam and tugged it the remainder of the way apart. When both ears were separated from the stuffed toy's head, she tossed everything but them to the floor.

Reggie walked to the mirror. Inspecting the destruction, she selected two long, sharp slivers and pried them loose from the frame. She slipped the pointy end into one cloth ear until the tip cut a small hole in the end and stuck out a few inches. She secured stuffing and the open end of the ear around the thicker portion of the shard. That should protect her hand. Picking a couple of hair elastics up from the floor, she wrapped them around that thick edge. Completing the same process with the second piece, she had created two knives.

She slipped one into the pocket of her jacket. Lifting her right leg, she wasn't surprised to discover her knife sleeve empty. She slid the second blade into it. It was obvious from the weight her pistol had also been removed from the leg holster on her other leg. Likewise, they'd taken the small automatic pistol she wore beneath her bra.

Reggie removed her blazer and carefully placed it on the bed, leaving the armed pocket toward herself, in case she needed it. She took her tank top off and unbuckled the beneath-the-bra handgun holder. She slid the holster off its belt and put it in her empty jacket pocket. Donning the tank, she put her navy blazer back on. She secured the ends of the holster belt ends together with the buckle then stretched it tight between her hands, evaluating its strength. It would do for a garrote.

Armed and dangerous, she gazed around the room, looking for anything else that might give her leverage against the Knapps. She picked up the chair and placed it behind where the door would open as their kidnapper entered. She was a tad shorter than Nathan, so standing higher on the chair might enable her to take him down more easily.

She knelt beside the bed. "I'm ready. Now we need to figure out how to get you loose." She inspected the lock mechanism around Blare's ankle. "Does it hurt?"

Blare's head tilted and the closest shoulder rose toward it and fell. "Yeah, sometimes, when I pull against it; and it rubs."

Reggie carefully moved the locked side toward her. The chain was attached to it with a c-shaped bolt, and a padlock hung from it. The chain's other end was welded to the metal foot of the bed. Not easily removed.

Reggie's think, brunette curls were falling carelessly from her mussed French bun at the back of her head. She pulled the pins out and laid them on the bed beside Blare. Using one, she fumbled with the lock. She didn't find the release on the first try. On the third, a tiny snap sounded; and the lock fell open in her hand. Her training had once again come into play.

She wrapped a gentle hand around the girl's thin leg, pulled the white anklet down and checked her skin. It was red and hand signs of healing blisters, with stains on the sock where fluid had drained and thickened. She carefully pulled it back up without giving Blare a chance to view it.

"You're good as new. That ankle will forget it was ever here in a couple days." She willed God to bless Blare with a similar forgetfulness, hoping this episode didn't leave permanent emotional damage to the child.

She lifted Blare from the bed and gave her a big hug. "I don't know about you, Blare; but I need a hug right now."

Blare's tiny arms linked around Reggie's shoulders, and she gripped her tight. "Yeah, me too."

They stood that way for a few minutes. Neither acted eager to end the embrace. Reggie soaked in the fresh, clean smell only a child could have. She allowed Blare's curly locks to blanket her face, breathing in their soft fragrance.

Finally, she pulled back from the girl. "Let's go check on something." She sat Blare on her stocking feet and picked up the dress Blare had worn earlier. "Mind if I use this?"

Blare snickered. "Heck no. I hate that gross thing. They took my clothes. She said they were indecent."

Reggie had read the report and talked over and over with the mother. Blare had been wearing a blue, floral tank top, a pair of navy shorts, pink socks and pink, light-up sneakers. Nothing indecent about that.

She ripped the skirt from the bodice of the dress and tore it in two pieces. Wrapping one around each of her feet, she pulled ends together and tied them in front of her ankles. "There, now I have fancy socks too." She chuckled.

The little girl laughed along with her. "You look hilarious."

Reggie struck an exaggerated model pose. "I'll have you know, Miss Blare, this is the latest fashion people are raving about."

Together they giggled. It was the mood she'd hoped to instill in the child. Picking up the makeshift bat and taking Blare's hand, she led her to behind the door. "Let's hang out here awhile. If you hear any noise coming from the door, I want you to stay back against this wall and behind me." She patted the solid wall. "If I get into a fight with Mr. or Mrs. Knapp, you find a way to sneak through the door. Then just keep running. Don't stop until you get somewhere safe."

"Okay." Blare nodded.

"I'm going to try to pick this lock, but it's not going to be easy. It might take a while." Hinges were on the outside, and there was no place to stick a key into from this side. The only help were two screws holding it to the door.

She knelt in front of it and used the hair pins first. There wasn't enough leverage for her to twist the tight screws loose. She tried first one shard of glass then the other. After fiddling with the screws around a half an hour, they were as tight as ever.

Magnolia Blossoms

A sound came from the other side of the lock—a jingle and scrape of keys. He was back. "Remember what I told you. The girl stood and moved to stand with her back against the wall.

Reggie climbed onto the chair and poised. Holding the chair leg with the bolt sticking out of the top, above her head, she readied to slam it down with all her might on, what she hoped to be and unsuspecting, Nathan Knapp.

CHAPTER 25

Wyatt entered the viewing room as the deputy he sent to the interrogation room led Marianne Knapp out, to put the handcuffed perpetrator in her cell. Jaiden and Shea sat in chairs facing the door.

Jaiden leaned forward. "I've got something, Sheriff."

Wyatt took a seat facing them. "And?" He was never one to spare words.

"And . . . I searched the property database for the name Knapp but came up with nothing. Expanding the search to include Marianne Knapp's given name, Harold, and Nathan's mother's maiden name of Carroll, I found a property in Sweetwater County left for Marianne Knapp by her parents. Marianne never bothered to put it in her own name. It's a ten-acre parcel at the end of a dead-end, two-mile-long road with only one other home on the lane. According to the county's records, there is a house on the property. It was built in the 1920s, so may be dilapidated . . . or not."

Wyatt's stony face broke into a sly grin. "That's where they're holding them. I'll bet money on it."

Magnolia Blossoms

Shea's phone signaled in his hand. He glanced at it. "It wouldn't be this location? Would it?" He turned the screen toward Jaiden.

Her dark head nodded, and she grinned. "Absolutely. How did you know?"

"Reggie has a tracking device on her. She always wears it, in case of emergency. Because of her role with the FBI, she can't have it turned on all the time. I've been trying like hell to pick up her signal, assuming she would've turned it on if she was in danger. I couldn't get anything until just now."

"Why would it just now come on?" Wyatt's forehead scrunched, forming tiny lines across it beneath his silver hair.

Shea shrugged. "I'm not sure. Maybe she was somewhere that the signal couldn't get out of. Or she just now turned it on. I don't give a damn. I just want to get the hell over there and bring my woman home."

"We're with you." Wyatt stood and the two followed him out of the room. "Jaiden, text Leo and let him know we're moving the party there. He and his crew should stay posted at the Knapp place, in case Nathan returns."

Shea led the way down the basement stairs of the dilapidated house on Marianne Knapp's inherited property. Wyatt followed close behind, lingering at the bottom of the rickety staircase. Jaiden stood guard upstairs. Their firearms were drawn.

Mildew scent filled the thick air. Their footsteps had left prints among others on the wooden steps. Cobwebs hung undisturbed from rotting rafters that supported the one-story, abandoned shack.

The rock-walled, dirt-floored, cellar-type basement had a concrete wall along one side. A steel door hung in the middle of it. Shea inspected the door frame and lock. If he couldn't pick the lock, he'd have to pry hinges off. One way or another, he was getting inside.

He knelt and pulled out his lock picking kit. He inserted a tool, put his ear to the mechanism and listened as he twisted, poked, pulled and turned. Finally, it gave way with a snap. He stuffed the tools in the kit and shoved it into his utility belt.

Nathan could be inside with them. Or he could be long gone. If that was the case, would he have disposed of them first?

A shiver sped down Shea's neck and back. He shook it off and redrew his automatic pistol. Poised to open the door, he said a silent prayer, they wouldn't find Reggie and Blare dead.

He signaled to Wyatt. With Wyatt's returned nod, Shea twisted the knob with his left hand, weapon in his right. He eased the door open.

"Reggie."

Swoosh. A gust of wind flew past his head. A club of some sort barely missed him, as it flew in front of his face.

Whack. The offending item struck the bed.

Reggie jumped down from atop a chair, where she'd been standing behind the door. Her arms were around his neck before her feet hit the floor. Her slight weight threw him sideways in surprise.

His hands steadied her, grabbing her rump and pulled her close. She smelled of gardenias and her unique personal scent. He soft, lips greedily played hard kisses across her face.

She spoke as she kissed him, "Damn it, Shea. I thought you'd never find me. I almost killed you. If you hadn't said my name as you opened that door, I wouldn't have diverted that blow."

He savored her soft curves, melting against him. Having feared the worst, he was flooded with relief, and held her so close she nearly became part of him. Had he lost her for good, he'd never be whole again.

He should've known. If there was any way possible, Reggie would find a means to escape captivity and rescue Blare. Or, she'd have fought to the death.

That shiver sensation paraded down his spine again. Had Reggie encountered Nathan with her blow, she would now be in a battle for her life.

Wyatt walked into the room and around the canoodling couple. He bent his long frame to come eye-to-eye with the tiny girl cowering against the wall. "Hello. I'm Sheriff Wyatt. That's Reggie's husband, Marshal Montgomery. I suppose you're Miss Blare Moore. We've come to take you home."

Blare took the huge hand Wyatt extended to her. Her tiny one looked like that of a miniature porcelain doll enveloped in his. She wrapped her fingers around his as best they could fit and mimicked a shake, she'd undoubtedly witnessed by other adults in the past.

"Nice to meet you, Sheriff. That's my friend, Reggie."

Reggie pried herself from Shea's grasp and knelt to face her. "Wyatt, this is my partner, Blare." She put a hand up.

Blare slapped it with her palm. "Yeah, we're partners."

Shea chuckled from behind them. "How about we take your partner home?" He stooped, and with a motion from Reggie, Brea climbed on his back. "Hang on there, partner." He stood and took Reggie's hand and led her out of the room she'd been confined in with Blare early afternoon. Poor Brea had been held there for three weeks and a day.

As they climbed the dusty staircase, he and Blare following Reggie's round behind rocking side-to-side up the steps, it set in how he'd almost lost the most precious part of his life. A rock lodged in his throat then he recalled. "Hey, Babe, we'll have to jog about a half mile down the road to the neighbor's house. We left Jaiden's squad car parked behind their garage and told them a fugitive was on the loose, to stay inside with their doors locked.

"I don't give a darn if we have to jog all the way home." Her smiling face beamed over her shoulder.

Walking through the falling-down structure, the clear night provided a magnificent array of stars lit by a full moon. Jaiden pulled their vehicle to the front gate. "Ya' all need a ride?" She left the motor running, jumped out of the driver's side and rounded the automobile. "She's all yours."

"How did you get it here so fast?" He stared at the stunning half-Irish, half-Choctaw, pint-sized deputy. "I heard from my post it was just Reggie and Blare in the room. Wyatt had your back, so I ran down to get you a ride." She hugged Reggie, and the women clung together for a long moment. "You scared us shitless, gal."

Reggie broke away from her friend with a grateful smile. "Sorry about that. Thanks for rescuing us." Reggie climbed into the passenger seat.

Shea handed her the drowsy child. "It won't hurt to break the rules this once. I don't have the nerve to put this little one in the back seat. She'd probably rather you hold her, partner."

Blare's sleepy head nodded. She curled into Reggie's arms and fell instantly asleep.

"We'll be right back." Seated in the driver's chair, Shea bent his tall head to view Jaiden through the passenger side window.

Magnolia Blossoms

Her head rocked in recognition. "Thanks. The Sheriff and I will get things set up. Let's catch this prick." Probably realizing her language wasn't fit for use in front of a child, she glanced at the girl in Reggie's arms.

"No worries." Reggie waved her away. "She's out like a New York City gutter drunk on a Saturday night binge."

The drive to the Moore's residence took only fifteen minutes. Shea parked in front of their house, came around and opened the door for Reggie, then sped ahead to ring the doorbell. The house was dark, but a light instantly flashed on in the living room. A second later, Ryan Moore swung the door open, looking haggard, unshaven with bags under his too-young-to-have them eyes. He clearly hadn't been sleeping, or he wouldn't have turned the light on so quickly, but the plaid shorts and tee shirt he wore looked as though they'd been slept in for days.

Quickly scrambling in, probably from her bedroom, came Twila. Her hair was mussed, and she wore no makeup. Her eyes were puffy, as though she'd been trying to cry herself to sleep but failed.

The parents had a look of trepidation and shock on their worried faces. Brows wrinkled, Twila bit her lower lip and twisted a loose tendril of hair. Ryan self-consciously pulled at the skin at the front of his neck. His shaggy hair, now his norm, appeared to have been unwashed for several days.

He cleared his throat, clasped hands together in front of him and asked with a watery gaze, "Have you found something?"

Shea smiled, feeling his wife's presence as she carried her bundle to stand behind him. Shea stepped aside. Reggie walked up the two steps and handed her load into the waiting and tearfully eager arms of her mother.

Twila gasped, and with shaky laughter carried her daughter to the closes chair then slumped into it holding Blare close to her chest. Ryan's hand flew to cover his mouth. Removing it, his face went into a slow smile. He walked to squat beside his wife and daughter. With a trembling hand, he ran a finger across Blare's cheek.

Blare's eyes widened, and she smiled the biggest smile one could imagine on her tiny face. "Mommy, Daddy, am I really home?"

"You are my sweet baby." Twila back handed a stream of tears from her cheek, but the flow wasn't dissuaded. "I'm so happy you're home safely."

"My partner, Reggie, promised she'd bring me home." Her head popped up, and she glanced around then smiled when her gaze met Reggie's. "Thank you, Reggie."

Shea's eyes teared up watching the family, so engrossed in their joy they seemed to have forgotten the law officers in their living room at two a.m.

"You're very welcome, partner. We make a wonderful team. I couldn't have done it, without your help. Mr. and Mrs. Moore, your daughter is a very brave girl, and she's a hero in this story." Reggie's eyes filled with moisture. She sniffed and reached for Shea's hand.

Her small, soft palm quivered in his big mitt, as he gripped it firmly. "We'd best get back to work and let you folks get some sleep. Lock your doors. We'll check back with you sometime tomorrow."

Ryan followed them to the door. His whisper was meant only for Shea and Reggie, not to be heard by his family. "Did you get the SOB who took her?"

Shea gave him one of his practiced faces. The kind you used when not wanting to scare someone too much, but also not wanting to lie. "We have apprehended one of the two parties we believe were involved and expect to bring the other fugitive in within the next twenty-four hours. Don't worry about them. We've got this. He's not likely to come after Shea or bother ya' all again. Take care of your family. We'll do the rest." Shea turned and put an arm around his wife's shoulders. The door clicked locked behind them.

Moments later they parked Jaiden's work vehicle behind the neighbor's barn where they'd hid it previously. Shea popped the trunk and pocketed the keys.

He tossed Reggie her flak jacket. "I figured you'd need this."

"Thanks." Leave it to her efficient hubby to be prepared.

While she slipped into it, he brought out her favorite work boots. "I love the new fashion trend you're trying to set, but you might want to change into these.

"How did you know?" She zipped the jacket closed and bent to untie the bindings over her feet, having completely forgotten about them.

"Found your heels in the backseat of your car."

"Huh, I figured them for a lost cause. Thought Knapp would toss 'em into a dumpster or something."

"Probably didn't want to take the time." Shea's lean, solid frame leaned a hip against the fender. His eyes never moved from her as she exposed her bare feet and slipped into the socks and boots, he'd brought her.

"That's great. Damned shoes cost almost a week's pay, and they were my favorites." She stood tall as her petite physique could.

"A week's pay?" He stood up and began pulling weapons from the trunk. "I borrowed the fire power from the Sheriff's office. Figured they'd disarm you."

"Yeah, Nathan took me by surprise. Injected something in my neck. I didn't even know he'd come home. Next thing I knew, I was trussed up like a Thanksgiving turkey. Lying on my ass. Propped in a corner of that freaky dungeon with a major hangover. No shoes. No weapons."

"You must've suspected something. You did leave the phone on record in their couch. Wyatt's team tracked you there. Then zilch."

She unzipped the top of her vest and shoved the Colt M4 carbine into her cleavage. "I didn't trust Marianne, and by the time we'd talked a few minutes, I knew she was involved. Not sure if it'll stand up in court, but I figured taping the rest of our conversation might help us locate Blare. He must've snuck in when I was checking the rest of the house out. He came up from behind me. As I felt his presence, the needle went in, and I shoved the cell between the cushions."

Shea handed her a long blade. She bent and placed it into her empty calf holder. It wasn't her favorite, but it would do. She took the utility belt from Shea and buckled it around her waist then checked the ammo in the Glock 19 he gave her and place it in the holster at her right hip. She tossed her blazer in the back with a clank. "Shit, I forgot about the shivs I crafted from the mirror."

Shea chuckled, lifting out the makeshift weapons with his fingers. "Deadly. I should've figured."

She shrugged with a head tilt sideways. "A girl's got to have her stuff."

He bent and kissed her lips, tenderly at first, as his long fingers thread through her hair. She stood on tiptoes to meet him full tilt. His breath was hot and smoldering firing every hormone bouncing around in her hungry body. She drew in his probing tongue and languished in a pleasure she'd figured to never have again. Her leg came up to curl around his, as he squatted slightly to push his manhood against her melting crux. Their body armor separated them, reminding her they had other priorities now. Her libido could wait.

"Slow down, lover boy. Work first. Then you can spend the next few days scratching the itch in my groin."

"Days?" He chuckled pulling away from her to raid the trunk once again.

"Yeah, I figure it'll take at least that long to satisfy my need to feel alive. You're the best cure I know for what ails me."

"You've got it, boss." He tossed her a Remington 700 sniper rifle and selected a Remington 870 12-gauge shotgun for himself. He shut the trunk with a quite snap.

"You know me well, my husband." She checked the rifle's ammo and hung the sling across her shoulder. "Ready for a short hike through the woods?" They didn't dare take the road, since Knapp would drive along it if he was to return. "What are the chances he's already arrived?"

"About fifty-fifty, I'd guess." Shea fell into step beside his wife, and they trotted soundlessly as possible through the forest alongside the dirt road.

CHAPTER 26

Reggie was posted inside the room with Wyatt. The door had been fixed to appear locked when it was not. Shea stood guard hidden beneath the basement staircase, in a cubbyhole that opened to the other side, so he wasn't visible to someone descending or approaching the door to the secret room. Jaiden watched the road from her position inside the woods across from the house. Leo and his team remained at the Knapp residence, in case Nathan returned there first.

APBs were out on Knapp's truck, and his employer had been notified to contact the Sheriff's Department, should he show up at work. Nothing was out of place in the ramshackle house, inside or out.

It was nearing dawn and hours had gone by before Jaiden's soft Texas twang came over their coms. "Knapp's truck's coming down the lane." The plan was she'd wait until he'd gone inside the shack then disable his vehicle in case, he got a chance to run.

Soon, she came again. "He's in. Get ready. Truck's unlocked." The click of the vehicle's hood release sounded. Then Jaiden's mike went quiet.

Seconds later the Knapp's key sounded as it was inserted into the door slot. Wyatt faced the door, pistol aimed directly ahead. Reggie stood to his right weapon pointed the same direction. Seconds later, a scratching sounded, as Knapp's key was inserted in the slot.

Magnolia Blossoms

Wyatt's long leg shot forward, kicking the door open outward. A thud came as steel slammed into their visitor. Knapp's body came into view, flailing backward trying to regain his stance. His right hand held a revolver. He swung around, clearly, to escape.

Shea blocked his path to the stairs, his automatic pointed at the man's chest. Wyatt's foot slammed into the back of Knapp's knee, sending him sprawling to the left. As he fell, three shots rang out simultaneously. Reggie had fired one at Knapp striking his left shoulder. The other two came from Knapp's and Shea's weapons.

Wyatt fell to a kneel atop the backside of a prone Knapp. Blood pooled around the fallen man. Reggie leaped past them, as Wyatt shoved Knapp's gun aside, grabbed his wrists and snapped handcuffs to hold them behind Nathan's rear.

She squatted in front of her husband. Shea's head lolled to the side. He laid unconscious, back to the staircase. Legs spread out in front of him toward her. She stowed her weapon in its holster and took his face in her hands. His pulse was strong against her fingers. As her face drew near his, he was not breathing.

She gently slapped at his cheek. "Wake up, Shea. Breathe, damn it." Her urgent fingers fumbled with the straps holding his protective gear tight against his torso. She stretched him gently onto his back, preparing to give him CPR.

Jaiden spoke from where she assessed the scene from the top of the stairs, having rushed to help with the take down. "Officer down. Two injured. Need two ambulances STAT." Her voice trailed off as she walked back upstairs and gave the dispatcher the location.

Shea's eyes popped wide, and a look of shock came over his face. A sudden gasp inhaled air into his empty lungs. It edged its way out again. Then he drew a hearty second breath in and out, and in again. "What the hell?" He puffed air out with an 'o'-shaped lips.

Finally able to breath herself, Reggie smiled. "You trying to scare the daylights out of me, Montgomery? You took a round in that battle." Her hands wildly played across his chest and flat, hard stomach. "No blood."

"Ouch, woman, watch it." He jerked when her hand touched a rib.

"Lay still, baby. You might have a cracked rib. No sense causing further damage." She felt the front of his flak jacket. "Here's the bullet. Your vest stopped it. Looks like Remington .40-gauge metal jacket. Hot damn. That could've been bad."

Shea snickered attempting to sit up. "Babe, you know I'm ten-feet-tall and bulletproof."

Her gentle hand pushed him back. "Easy, cowboy. This isn't a country music video, and you're not moving until the EMT's take you away."

"Believe me, it's no picnic even with protective gear."

Reggie leaned forward and kissed his soft lips. "You're going to be okay, Shea. I need you to be okay."

"Another kiss like that would help," he whimpered, and she awarded him his request.

Jaiden stepped around them to where Wyatt knelt beside his captive. He lifted Knapp slightly to gander at his wounds. "Two shots."

"Yours, Sheriff?" Jaiden stared then bent to pick up Knapp's handgun, using an evidence bag she pulled from her rear pocket.

"No, I didn't fire. They're from Reggie and Shea." He stood beside his deputy.

Sirens approached from a short distance.

"I'll go outside and direct everyone. Leo and his team are on the way to help gather evidence here. After the

EMTs arrive, I'll run and get our vehicle. I'll stow this in the trunk." She held up Knapp's plastic-wrapped revolver.

"Good, thanks for calling Leo." Wyatt strode to their friends.

Jaiden looked at Shea and Reggie. "Glad you were wearing a vest." She started climbing the dusty stairs.

"Yes, and thanks to Wyatt for throwing Knapp off balance. That close, Knapp could've landed a head shot." Reggie finally allowed emotion to sift through the shell of her professional demeanor, and her eyes glazed over with moisture.

CHAPTER 27

Two days later, Wyatt strolled onto the deck of his and Sage's home, a modified A-frame, cedar and glass house, set secluded from Paradise Way by woods surrounding the ten-acre farm. Three horses grazed in a pasture to the right and in front of a black wooden barn. Sage's ex-police German Shepherd, Tuffy, romped playfully with Wyatt's cocker spaniel, Belle, in the front yard.

Wyatt handed three beers to his wife and guests, then took a seat beside Sage. "Glad you're feeling better, Shea. That round you took could've easily done more damage than a bruised rib and liver."

"Yeah, thanks, pal; but it was no fun pissing blood for the last few days." Shea chuckled.

"I'm just glad we caught those monsters." Reggie sighed.

Sage watched their youngster, Ty, being chased by the dogs after snatching away the stick they'd been playing with. Ty giggled, spun and tossed the branch, sending the animals scurrying after it. "I can't imagine harming a child."

"Yeah, me either." Reggie took Sage's hand from where they sat beside each other. "You don't need to worry about the Knapps any longer. Nathan never made it to the hospital alive, and Marianne is going to spend the rest of her days in lockup—or worse."

Magnolia Blossoms

Sage breathed out a gush. "So, Wyatt tells me you two are back in Sweetwater for good."

Shea nodded a decisive head. "We are."

"So, what do you think of purchasing the property we talked about?" Sage winced and took a sip of her beer. "I know it's got a taint on it, with those poor girls being found buried there. Does it hold such horrible memories for you two, you've decided against it?"

Shea and Reggie glanced at each other then back at their friends. Reggie shrugged. "Not entirely. We've seen it all, in our years working law enforcement. Can't hold it against the land, that a crime was committed there."

Shea sat his bottle down. "Actually, the murders were committed on Marianne Knapp's property. The girls were given decent burials on that land."

Wyatt's face went into a broad smile. "I was hoping you would feel that way. I reached out to the heirs again. As you know, none of them have been in town for about thirty years. After their dad died, they let the house fall into dilapidated condition. It eventually collapsed in bits and pieces. The grown children and grandchildren live all over the world. The estate executor contacted them all. None of them have any interested in it, especially now, with victims of a multiple homicide have been unearthed there. They offered us a deal I don't think we can afford to pass up. He sent it in writing." Wyatt pulled the offer from his pocket and handed the papers to Reggie.

She and Shea read over the contract. Her mouth gaped open, and she met Shea's emerald green eyes. "Babe?"

He nodded.

"This is some deal." Reggie scrunched her nose up.

Sage nodded. "Yes, it is. The owners believe the property is untouchable, and they look at us as their only way of unloading an undesirable property. If they ever want to get anything at all from it, they figure we're their only chance to unload it."

Wyatt grinned, making those sexy dimples appear in his square jaw. "Sage and I had talked about making them a low-ball offer, but the conversation never got that far. The story was on the national news, and I guess they were concerned about the land's value. Before I could offer, he told me he was emailing me their contract for consideration."

Sage beamed. "What do you think?"

Fluttering in her gut told her this was it—what she and Shea had longed for—a chance to start over in Sweetwater, for good this time. "We'd be damned fools to pass this up. Splitting the farm with you two is a dream come true. I'm home to stay. We're going to build a new house on a beautiful piece of property. Our next-door neighbors are our best friends. How could life get any better?"

Her biological clock banged loudly and clearly in her head. She shot a glance at Ty, giggling and playing with the dog. She stood and gripped the railing, longing on her face.

Sage stood and slid an arm around her shoulders. "Think you and Shea can stop getting shot at long enough to spit one of those out for yourselves?"

She snickered and pecked her best girl pal on the cheek. "Why should we? If I recall, you got shot at while you were pregnant."

Sage rolled eyes heavenward and released her, spinning to face her husband. "You had to bring that up."

Wyatt laughed and glared at Shea. "I do believe it won't be the jobs that kill us. These women are going to be the death of us."

Shea chuckled as he stood to hug his wife. "You've got that right, old buddy."

THE END

Magnolia Blossoms

Dear Reader,

If you liked the Reggie Chronicles, Hart's Girl #1, Heart of the Matter #2, and Magnolia Blossoms #3, you're going to love reading more from Lynda Rees. Her next book is Flip or Flop, Murder House. Here's a FREE chapter sample to get you started.

FLIP OR FLOP MURDER HOUSE

CHAPTER 1

Charli Owens strode a few feet from her pickup to where the auction would be held. A few characters she knew casually waited for the Sheriff and County Clerk to exit the Sweetwater courthouse. A couple of insurance agents, a boring, grey-suited guy studying his clip board—a bank representative monitoring the sale, and an older couple, made up the group.

A pickup truck with ladder racks on top pulled to the curb and stopped. Buckets and equipment filled the bed—a contractor's work vehicle. A too-hot-to-be-loose on the street guy stepped out of the driver's side and rounded the truck.

Trouble.

Shaggy blonde hair draped his neck, framing a swoon-worthy face. Light eyes glowed from his smile, noticeable from the distance. It lit up his face, causing adorable wrinkles at their sides. A slim waist joined long, slender legs in tight-fitting jeans. He dwarfed the petite, blonde with cropped locks, who climbed from the passenger side.

The female reached in and helped a miniature version of her out.

Bouncing red curls topped the toddler's head, and she wore overall blue jeans with a red tee shirt. Her father took her hand. The mom tiptoed to kiss his cheek, bent to do the same to their daughter then strolled around, jumping into the driver's seat then sped away.

Lovely family. No danger there.

A pang hit Charli's heart, having hoped to have a household like that by now.

Hunky Daddy ambled slowly, so his daughter could keep up as they walked. Petite like her mother, the imp looked about four or five. Dad stood six-feet-four inches tall at least, probably more like six-foot-six. Broad shoulders strained fabric of his black tee stretching across a rolling chest and rippling abs.

Stopping at the rock wall by the courthouse steps, he squatted and whispered to the little one. She slipped behind him, and tiny arms surrounded his neck. He grasped the pudgy hands, lifted her onto his back then positioned himself to allow her to step onto the wall. She sat with legs dangling. He hopped to land beside her and put an arm across her shoulders, giving her a sweet hug.

Charli pushed away jealousy gnawing at her and waltzed toward a familiar couple. "Hi, Sandy, Mike. Are you looking to buy?"

Twenty-something Mike Carey shook her hand. "Not sure we're in position to purchase at auction."

Sandy Carey slid a palm across her protruding tummy and shook Charli's hand "Mike and I don't understand the process."

Mike nodded. "We decided to observe, though we'd love to bid on the Blossom Lane house."

Charli swallowed a lump lodged in her throat. "You aren't swayed by—"

Magnolia Blossoms

Mike interrupted her bumbling attempt at posing the question tactfully. "Not a bit. It had nothing to do with us."

Charli exhaled relief and inhaled hope, nodding at Sandy's belly. "Congratulations, I didn't realize you were expecting. Is that why you're in the market?" There was the green-eyed monster again. Charlie pushed it down.

Sandy beamed. "Our daughter is coming in September. We've prequalified for an FHA mortgage, but there's nothing on the market we're interested in. Blossom would fit us well, but we're not sure about tackling a fixer upper."

Mike's faced reddened. "I'm not helpless, but a lot needs to be done to that house. You're an expert and a real estate agent. Maybe you can help." He pulled out a paper and handed it to Charli. "This is our mortgage approval letter."

Relieved she wouldn't need to compete with the young couple for the property, she reviewed the document then handed it to Mike. "You won't be able to purchase a house needing renovation. FHA strenuously inspects your purchase to ensure it won't require major improvements for a long while. They don't want to put you in a position where they might need to foreclose."

Mike solemnly nodded. "I was afraid of that."

Charli smiled warmly. "I'm bidding on that property for my next rehab."

Sandy frowned. "Don't you remodel more expensive houses?"

Charli put a happy face on. "I'm taking the company in a different direction. There's a vast market for reasonably priced housing." They didn't need to know about Charli's effort to salvage her company and make a mark on her own.

Mike folded the sheet and stuck it in his pocket. "We're having trouble finding a suitable home."

"If I'm successful and get Blossom Lane, my intention is to bring it to perfect condition. I'll give you first crack at it if you want."

Sandy's eyes grew wide. "Yes, absolutely, we want to take a look when you're ready."

Mike grinned at his wife then turned to Charli. "Thank you. That would be perfect."

Charli cocked her head and eyed the handsome father and his child. She had hoped to be the only contractor bidding. "Pray I win at auction."

The strange man's head lifted, allowing a better view of his face. A square jaw eased into a grin, showing off glistening whites. Amusement appeared in almost iridescent gray eyes. Tiny wrinkles formed on outsides as he nodded pleasantly in Charli's direction.

Damn. She'd been caught gawking. Just what a good-looking guy needed, a stroke to his ego.

The antique, double doors opened. Sheriff Wyatt Gordon stepped out with a woman. He scanned and welcomed the crowd, introduced himself and the clerk and explained the process. The auction began.

An agent Charli recognized purchased a couple of city plots for his out-of-town insurance company. Bidding started for a laundromat. The older couple upped the banker's offer. A man in a business suit made a competing proposal. They countered a couple of times until he gave a resolved shake of his head.

Hunky Daddy sat quietly observing. That didn't bode well in Charli's mind. She'd hoped to avoid competition. His vehicle screamed contractor, someone who might bid against her. Blossom was the only property left.

Charli took a final look at figures in her notebook, reminding herself to stay within budget. She'd carefully inspected the house earlier in the week, gotten accurate pricing data together and assessed renovated value based on market data. Her bottom dollar was enough to satisfy the mortgage holder. It might not stand up against an aggressive bidder.

This guy better not be here for her house. The place had good bones. She needed it to keep her company afloat but didn't have money to get into a bidding war, not if she planned to keep a cushion to deal with unforeseen issues.

It wasn't simply her need to eat and provide shelter for her family. Self-esteem had suffered a deafening blow during dissolution of her partnership. Her pride was the size of a two-penny nail.

Damn it to hell.

That son of a bitch, Thompson Shade, wasn't about to end her. Shoulders rocked back. Her chin shot high. Resolve eased her rigid jaw.

She'd bought many a house at auction, designed, remodeled and successfully sold million-dollar residences at major profits. This dinky, three-bedroom pit wasn't about to get the better of her.

Wyatt opened the bid. The bank rep's hand shot up. The elderly couple upped the price a thousand dollars. Charli's hand went high, accepting the auctioneer's offer a thousand more. Next submission increased another grand. Hunky Daddy's mitt rose into the air. Charli took the next grand. The old couple's eyes met, and they dropped out. Hunky Daddy and Charli went up a thousand a time, playing against each other.

Charli gaped at her scratchpad. She lifted her paw and shouted a proposition five-thousand dollars higher. Hunky Daddy grimaced then shrugged as he shook his head.

Wyatt's announced, "Sold to Charli Owens."

Relief flooded her lungs and swilled into her gut. She smiled pleasantly toward Hunky Daddy.

He'd already hopped down and was lifting his child to her feet. Without a gaze Charli's direction, he took the girl's hand; and they strolled from Town Square.

His fine ass moved side-to-side. Broad shoulders shifted with ease of his stride, as those lengthy legs took him and his daughter down the street. Sandy, shaggy hair was chin length and might look lazy on some men but enhanced sex appeal to a peak on this guy. She sighed when they rounded the corner and disappeared.

With nothing left to watch, Charli waltzed into the courthouse to finalize the deal. She'd searched the title, having done it many times before. Paying cash, the title company was prepared to close in three days.

Afterward on the street, Charli whipped out her phone and dialed. Her best gal pal, Jaiden. "So? Did you get it?" Deputy Jaiden Coldwater's Texas drawl was nearly identical to local, Kentucky twang.

Charli chuckled. "Yep, I figured Wyatt would've filled you in."

"Nope, information is confidential until closing. The boss said if you wanted me to know, you'd tell me. Congratulations. Your business is on track. We need to celebrate and then find you a decent fella. You need to get that fine tush of yours back out there." Since Jaiden had gotten engaged to handsome surgeon, Clay Barnes, she'd been on a mission to fix Charli up.

Charli's eyes shot toward the heavens. "Hell no; I've sworn off the male sex, at least until I finish this rehab and sell the property."

"Whatever you say, but you can't stay off the market for long. Your love life needs a total rebuild."

"Don't I know it. The finest male specimen I've seen in a long time showed up at the sale today. The dude was eye candy, palpitation worthy and sweating testosterone clear across the courthouse lawn. It literally made my thong wet when his dreamy peepers met mine. I was perspiring blood; my face went so red."

"You don't sound sure about this temporary-celibate thing." Jaiden chuckled. She hadn't masked her relief when Thompson had tossed Charli aside like yesterday's takeout, and she wasn't on board with Charli's *no men for a while* choice.

"Honey, I'm not dead. There's nothing wrong with my sight. I might not be shopping, but I can view the merchandise. That boy was too hot to ignore. I had to soak up some of that sex appeal while he was hanging around. I can tell you my libido is fully intact."

"So why didn't you hit that?"

Charli tucked away in her mind the male vision causing her to perspire like the morning dew. "The guy is taken, married. They have the most adorable, little girl."

"Got 'cha," Jaiden groaned. "Oh well, at least, what's his name hasn't ruined you for other men. There's a deserving, guy out there for you, Charli. You'll find him when you're ready. Speaking of ready, when are we going to celebrate?"

AUTHOR'S NOTE: Get *Flip or Flop, Murder House* at https://www.lyndareesauthor.com

Become a **VIP** and get a **FREE** copy of *Leah's Story*, Preamble to *The Bloodline Series.*
https://preview.mailerlite.com/t1a6j6

For more from this author, consult the list of published books in the following pages.

Magnolia Blossoms

ALSO BY LYNDA REES

Historical Romance:
Gold Lust Conspiracy
Mystery:
The Bloodline Series:
Leah's Story
Parsley, Sage, Rose, Mary & Wine
Blood & Studs
Hot Blooded
Blood of Champions
Bloodlines & Lies
Horseshoes & Roses
The Bloodline Trail
Real Money
The Bourbon Trail
Reggie Chronicles:
Hart's Girls, #1
Heart of the Matter, #2
Magnolia Blossoms, #3
Single Titles:
God Father's Day
Madam Mom
2nd Chance Ranch
Flip or Flop
7 Book Anthology: *Sacrifice For Love:*
Second Chance Romance, Lynda Rees
Children's Middle Grade:
Freckle Face & Blondie
The Thinking Tree
Children's Picture and Learning:
NO FEAR
No Fear Learning and Activity Book

Find information about these books at website:
http://www.lyndareesauthor.com

235

ABOUT LYNDA REES

Lynda is the Murder Guru, a storyteller, an award-winning novelist, and a free-spirited dreamer with workaholic tendencies and a passion for writing. Her dreams come true, blessing her with a supportive family. Whatever crazy adventure Lynda congers up, her loving Mike is by her side.

A diverse background, visits to exotic locations, and curiosity about how history effects today's world fuels her writing.

Born in the splendor of the Appalachian Mountains as a coal miner's daughter and part-Cherokee, she grew up in northern Kentucky when Newport prospered as a mecca for gambling and prostitution.

Lynda's work is published in cozy mystery, historical romance, children's middle-grade, non-fiction, advertising copy, self-help and freelance.

Author's Note:

I hope you enjoy my work and we become life-long friends.

Lynda Rees

Love is a dangerous mystery. Enjoy the ride!

Get the latest book deals, exclusive content, and **FREE** reads by joining my **VIPs**. Email me for a **FREE** copy of *Leah's Story* at https://preview.mailerlite.com/t1a6j6
Visit my website: http://www.lyndareesauthor.com
Email: lyndareesauthor@gmail.com

Lynda Rees